I0742210

Published by: Kendrai Meeks/Tulipe Noire Press

Text Design by: The Last TK

Edited by: Rebecca Hodgkins

Cover Design by: Mario Lampic

ISBN-10: 1-7337655-1-4

ISBN-13: 978-1-7337655-1-0

KENDRAI MEEKS

THE WOLF AND THE WATCHER

RED HOOD ORIGINS
BOOK TWO

Many of us live in dysfunctional families, and so even if it's in a fairy tale, or perhaps because it's in a fairy tale, we have a chance to look at that side of our reflected lives differently.

-Kenneth Branagh

ONE

Andreas Baron, konigswolf of the Schwarzwald pack, could split logs from Michaelmas until Christmas and still, the angst would remain.

Wilhem should not have been surprised, therefore, to find half of the fuel they'd need to make it through winter chopped and piled. What *did* surprise him was how his king achieved the work of three lupines in one night.

"Good health, *mein konig?*"

Andreas paused, the axe raised high, to glare at his packling. "Do you question my constitution?"

Wilhelm's eyes cast to the ground as his body curled in on itself. "No, Andreas, of course not."

Andreas let his tool fall to the ground and rounded. "Then what business?"

The packling dared a glance upward. "Lisi is asking you to come sup before she puts the pups to bed. It is nearly dawn."

"Give your mate my thanks, but I am not hungry."

"But, *mein konig*, you haven't eaten a proper meal in two days. Or did you sneak off to the forest to take down a few coneys again?"

The kingwolf huffed. "And if I did? Am I not a predator? Should I not eat of the land as a predator is wont to do?"

Lord forbid the konigswolf should think his prerogatives were being questioned twice in so many winks. "It is justified to draw from the world that which it gives willingly. But you are also a man, and a man needs rest. Even the Almighty allowed himself his due on the seventh day."

The Almighty had never had to fight off the urges of a full moon growing near while living in the shadow of the woman he loved. How long had it been since they'd spoken? A year? At least that long.

"It has been a long night. But there's still much wood left to split."

Wilhelm patted Andreas's shoulder. "We'll do it together tomorrow. Come along now, my king, or Lisi will have both of our paws in the trap."

Snap.

Wilhelm fell in behind his king as the sensation gripped them both: a lurch in the stomach, a buzz in the head. They were no longer alone, even though neither could spot their interloper through the nearby trees.

The wind shifted, carrying the scent of freshly cut pine and silver.

"Curse the devil! What do they want?" Wilhelm asked. "And just when we're about to bed down for the day!"

Andreas wondered as well, but knew no matter how much he hoped, it wouldn't be her. Gerwalta patrolled these woods now, as she'd done since they returned from Nurenmberg, but the one he loved could slide through the trees without being spotted. More likely it was Helga, the Matron's first-born daughter and heir apparent, dropping by for a weekly shake down.

"Go, Wilhem." Andreas pushed his packling toward the direction of the farm as he himself turned deeper into the forest. "I'll be along shortly. Tell Lisi I'll help square away the pups for bed."

"Just as long as you tell whatever red-hooded ninny this turns out to be that she ought come at a more decent hour." Wilhelm moved along, but called back over his shoulder. "Next time you're hunting about the forest, you ought to find one of them to eat. Do us all a favor."

Andreas cringed at the thought. Animal though he was, hunter though God had made him, he'd never partake of dark one flesh. As he made his way to the forest's edge, however, he did consider other things that he could do involving his mouth and one particular wolfsretter's skin.

The image in his mind knocked the wind from his lungs and put his heart into his manhood. He found himself arrested, struggling to forgo a much more pleasant projection of what lay before him than humiliation.

And then suddenly, he caught the sight of red hair blowing in the breeze.

"Resplendent."

The word leapt from his heart unto his lips before he could stop himself. His love stood before him in her warrior's cloak, a deep scarlet fabric that stood out against the snow-kissed monochromatic backdrop of the winter forest. A berry ripe for eating. A rose blooming among ruin, waiting to be picked.

She was not the same untried flower he'd journeyed across the land beside a year before. His love had passed from a young protégé barely come into her powers to hardened warrior of a wolfblood-hungry heritage. Her stoic resolve proved that the fantasies he'd entertained of their next encounter, one that began with her running into his arms and out of her clothing, were simply that—make believe.

"Herr Baron." Gerwalta's arm jerked into view from under the folds of her red cloak, bearing a scroll in her outreached hand. "I come on behalf of the Matron."

Formality was a cruelty for those who loved. It frosted the heart, chilled desires. Andreas found himself playing the role she'd forced him into.

Smile absconded, the wolf seized the paper, breaking the Matron's red wax seal. "It is an invitation to a ball."

Gerwalta met his raised eyebrow with silence.

"At Schloss Wolfsretter," he continued. Other details were brief, but that didn't make them any less curious. He pushed the scroll into a pocket in his coat. "Why is the Matron inviting me, a lupine, to a wolfsretter ball?"

"I do not question my mother's decisions. I cannot say." The first crack in her resolve emerged, and much to his dismay, it was to huff in frustration. "I was charged with delivering the invitation to you, Herr Konigswolf, and I have done so. If you wish to discuss that matter further, you may send word to my mother to…"

He caught her by the arm as she spun to leave. He'd have thought he'd kissed her, the way her body lit up at his touch, her cheeks blushing, her heart pounding.

All signs of attraction. But were not these also the signs of an oncoming attack?

Gerwalta fixed him with a poisonous glare. "You *will* unhand me, for your sake."

If she wished to hurt him, she could. Gerwalta wore no silver in plain sight, but a wolfsretter rarely did. Andreas had no doubt that with a flick of her fingers, the metal would leech from the hidden confines of her attire and burn rivers into his skin. Her touch was worth the pain.

Instead of moving away, Andreas stepped closer, bringing her back flush to his chest, his hand still clasped on her arm. "I would rather *hand* you, Walta. Excessively."

"I thought we settled this matter the last we met." Her words made the chill in the air feel warm by comparison.

"Only if by settling you mean that you asked me to do something abhorrent, and I refused." His mouth danced over the skin beneath her ear, and still, she did not move. "I will never mate another."

"Then you'll die alone and without an heir."

As soon as his lips closed over the juicy lobe of her ear, it was over. Andreas did not know when Gerwalta had moved, for every moment and every movement had taken on such a dreamy state, his being was liquid without fine borders. Only when her warmth was filled in by pockets of cold did he look up to find his hooded love peering down at him from the tree limbs above.

"Why torture yourself like this?"

"Tis you who tortures me, love." He opened his arms, beckoning her. "Your denial is the mace that strikes my flesh. Your absence, the chains that bind me to hope."

"Hope? To what end?" she spat back, stepping off the branch, drifting gracefully down with inhuman leisure. "Every word you utter of this love lunacy dips the quill to the inkwell from which your death warrant is written. For a whole year, I have left you be so that you may squelch this idiocy. Did you waste your time on fantastical dreams of reunion? Why are you so intent to die?"

"It is death for me *not* to love you. Walta, please…"

She didn't allow herself to touch ground, remaining in a hover, bobbing like a feather on the rippling stream. Nevertheless, when he stepped forward and took her gloved hands in his, though the conflict warred in her eyes, she gave no retreat.

"…I will have but one love and one mate, and it will be you."

"Please, stop." Her head lashed to the side. "I beg of you, forget me. Find another. Have a dozen pups and teach them well to fear my kind, as even I fear my own."

All his tenderness took flame. "Who do you fear? Has someone hurt you? Name her and I'll have her throat."

"Killing the Matron would only lead to the destruction of your whole pack."

Tentative words belied the fervor of injustice he felt. "Your own mother causes you injury? By what measure and with what purpose?"

"For the desire to see me wed, Herr Baron, and by whatever measure she deems necessary." Her hand fished into the hidden pocket on his chest, pulling out the very missive that had brought her back to the packlands. "Invitations are going out to houses from Eire to Anatolia. A call for the Matrons of each territory to send any eligible son who wishes to vie for my hand. From those, she will choose whomever she deems worthy, and my consort that man shall be."

"But…" Andreas's mouth went dry. In what terms could he object to such a disgrace? If the tongues of man had such words, he did not know them. "You love *me*."

"I am the daughter of the Red Matron. I love whomever she commands." Gerwalta elevated herself a little more. "Please, forget me. Come to the ball and let your silence be my favor. Do not give my mother any opportunity to question her dominance, and especially do not look at me the way you are now, or all will know your love for me. It is bad enough that I feel it even still."

Before she'd allow another moment of protest, Gerwalta disappeared into the virgin light of morn.

TWO

She made sure to put her feet back to solid ground the moment she'd gained a goodly distance. Then, she struggled to keep those feet pointing toward home. What a lamentable fool she'd been. She'd avoided Andreas Baron for a year *because* she feared seeing him would spark her feelings once more. When her mother had given her the invite to the ball, and the explicit instruction that *she* would be the one to deliver it to the konigswolf, she'd retaliated for the first time in her life.

"Why should I tolerate a werewolf at the ball? Do we mean to sicken my suitors?"

Gunda rubbed the crumbs from a bit of fruited bread from her fingers. "I agree, it's loathsome. But this is an occasion when many a bloodline's envoys will be watching for what kind of a family and daughter I'm offering in marriage. Having the konigswolf there, and assuring he demonstrates obedience, gives an opportunity for me to observe your suitors' reactions. I will choose a husband who delights in Baron's pain."

Even now, the thought turned her stomach. She hated to speculate on how her mother had planned for Andreas to "demonstrate obedience." The ball was still two months away; perhaps that would be enough time for her to wage a passive campaign? Her mother, however, was no fool. Would Gunda suspect the truth?

For the moment, Gerwalta resolved to pass the day in bed, entertaining happier imaginations. One of the few good things that came out of her experiences with Andreas Baron was the understanding that she liked kissing perfectly well.

Gerwalta was also willing to bet she'd find the other acts of lovemaking even more agreeable. As Gerwalta passed into the keep and overheard two of her siblings talking, her ear caught on her name, arresting her.

"… and I want to know why she gets to have a ball," Helga, her eldest sister, said. "Mother didn't feel the need to undertake such an elaborate affair for either of us."

Zelda, third-born daughter, clicked her tongue. "You know that Mother always intended Bernhard for Gerwalta, so that she could send them off to live in Bavaria and strengthen her eastern flank. But now, with Bernhard and Maria dead—"

Gerwalta winced at that, still wondering if she were somehow responsible for her great aunt's death. No one knew what was revealed by Maria when she'd been summoned to court. Gerwalta had been the one, however, to bring light to the plots of Maria's son, Bernhard, as well as the one to see to his death. Could have sparing Bernhard and dragging him back to the Schwarzwald had somehow exonerated her aunt? Or was Maria part of some grander conspiracy?

She'd never know. Maria had been relinquished of her powers by the Matron, and at some point shortly thereafter, was found dead in the castle. Had it been suicide or something more sinister? A plot devised and executed in the shadows so that Gunda could have plausible deniability? No one within the confines of Schloss Wolfsretter dared fret over the justice a relinquished should receive.

"Well, she needs to marry Gerwalta off to someone, doesn't she?" Zelda finished. "Now that Gretchen and Pierre have taken control of Maria's region, Mother can spread the influence of the House of Red beyond our little corner of the forest with the right match."

Helga hummed her agreement. "She still fears what has come from the east with the Ottoman advance. My silver says Gerwalta finds herself in the Balkans or even Anatolia come spring."

Zelda laughed. "Ah, just picture that! Our little sister, riding bareback and living in a yurt."

"Do they really live in yurts?" Helga's voice suggested both amazement and disgust. "Well, then, the House of Night is hardly better off than Andreas Baron, are they? At least the lupines here have a solid roof overhead."

"And cattle and sheep sleeping under their floorboards." Zelda gagged. "Can you imagine, the smell of their dung tickling your nose morning, noon, and night? It's bad enough when we have to get close enough to the lupines to smell *them*."

"Imagine what's like to be mated to one." The women fell silent for a moment. "Do you think they mate, you know, mixed?"

"Mixed?" Helga asked. "What do you mean? Man and woman? I should say so. They certainly have enough pups running around all the time, don't they?"

"No, I mean *mixed*. You know, whilst one of them is a beast and the other, laity. Animal upon man. Or perhaps, woman."

"Is it not bad enough they mate at all?" Helga returned. "In any case, I'm delighted mother agreed to my plan to invite the konigswolf to the ball. His farmer stupidity should make for entertaining times. Imagine *him* trying to dance the Volta!"

Gerwalta struggled to contain herself. She wanted to dart around the corner and lay into the pair of gossiping goats. Andreas Baron was *not* stupid. He was engaging, complex, compassionate… and a thousand other kinds of wonderful that they should wish of their own husbands.

Still, there was some truth to his being ignorant, though what shame there was in not knowing a thing because there wasn't a need, Gerwalta couldn't say. What use did Andreas have for court dances and wolfsretter etiquette? She herself had been drilled on such matter since infanthood and sometimes forgot protocol. But surely he could gain some elementary knowledge before the ball to avoid embarrassment if he were advised. *She* could even teach him the basics, a dance or two…

Though it would mean spending time with him, and *that* was where she'd be stupid. She'd barely avoided the temptation of his proximity as it was. She'd have thought a year spent afar would douse her passions. Or, at least, his, which burned hotter. No such luck. The only thing time had bought was tinder, and if allowed a single spark between them, they'd both combust.

Someone tapped the wolfsretter's shoulder from behind. "Fraulein?"

Gerwalta's pulse exploded. Not because of the castellan's presence, though she immediately chastised herself for being so wrapped up in her own thoughts she had not heard the laywoman's approach. Rather, because the chattering in the antechamber beyond had abruptly cut off, making her older sisters aware of an interloper handing on their every word.

"Therese." Gerwalta said as flatly as possible, pulling her cloak out of being. "What is it?"

Helga and Zelda by this time had gathered themselves and joined their youngest sibling in the hall, eyes narrowed, questioning without words what might have been overheard.

The castellan's eyes weighed down with annoyance. Half of Therese's gray hair came about from the bickering of the four daughters. The other half, from Helga's abuse.

"You mother is asking you to join her in the tower."

Helga cackled as Zelda gasped and Gerwalta blinked in confusion.

"What possible business could mother have with *Gerwalta* that would be worthy of visiting the tower?" the eldest asked.

Normally, Gerwalta would snap at such condescension. Respect her elder siblings though she must before their mother, when left to their own devices, every instigation was met with retaliation. *As though she considers me some sort of threat.* Gerwalta couldn't understand what had possessed the heir apparent. Perhaps if Helga knew Gerwalta could fly, there'd be cause, but she didn't. No one did.

Except Andreas.

Therese continued. "I am merely a servant to this house, Frau Helga. It is not my place to infer any of the Matron's business, nor is it *yours*."

Few in the castle could hope to talk down at one of the Faust women and get away with it, but Therese was castellan, her sole duty was to ensure the sanctity and security of Schloss Wolfsretter itself. If that meant keeping Helga's ego in check, so be it. She had the scars to prove she was willing to assume the risks.

Helga turned her eyes to the ground. "Apologies, Frau Sainte-Maire."

"Accepted. Now, Fraulein Gerwalta?" Theresa jerked her head to the left. "If you would, please follow me."

Schloss Wolfsretter, having been built on a cliff that rose high above the valley, had no need for a wider view than that afforded its locale. The purpose of its tower was not to keep watch over the outside world, but to draw the gazes of those within its walls. There were no stairs leading to its top, per se. Rather, there was only a corridor where stairs should be. Only the righteous could ascend, and only by the working of silver to create a walkway that pooled into existence before each step and disappeared in her wake. The effort to climb to the top took excessive amounts of concentration and no little amount of silver. Though in Gerwalta's case, that needn't be so. She could fly if she wanted, if she were fool enough to expose her secret.

She hoped what her sisters said was true, that her mother would choose a suitor for her who would take her far from the Schwarzwald. If she remained too close to Andreas, too many secrets could come to the light of day.

Finally etching out the last step, then reclaiming the silver and shaping it into a block she left at the landing, it was some shock that she found her mother's dining table set for dinner, and seated at it, a man with pale skin, eyes of coal, and cropped, ebony hair. Handsome? Perhaps, but in a subdued way. The looks were a ruse, she understood on some unconscious level. A beautiful trap. He smelled of threat, despite his humble musculature and lack of any visible weapon. No one mentioned a visitor. Would not her gossip-loving sisters have been clucking if they knew? How had he gotten into the tower without any of the wolfsretter below the wiser?

He rose when their eyes met, and Gerwalta pulled herself from distraction to bow her head in due diligence.

"My apologies for the interruption, Matron. I was told you wished to see me." She raised her head, moving concern from the stranger's presence to his purpose. "I did not know you were in audience."

"No need for apologies, Gerwalta. I meant for you to meet." The Matron deposited her stein on the table as she gathered to her feet. "Spatar Goran Karahan, I present my fourth-born daughter, the Righteous Gerwalta Faust of Red."

Her official title? So rare were the occasions, she'd forgotten the proper decorum. Should she, like the laity, curtsey? She didn't wear a dress, unless one counted the bottom edge of a tunic as skirting. Opting for wolfsretter etiquette, Gerwalta crisscrossed her arms tight into her chest and stepped one foot behind the other. No sooner had she endeavored to undertake the gesture, however, then she was stopped by Karahan's sudden appearance right before her.

Gerwalta leapt back, instinctively drawing a weapon into being.

Karahan's hands went out wide, showing empty palms. "Peace, Fraulein. I thought you perceived my nature and would know of my manner. I did not attend to frighten you."

"You…" She swallowed, hoping to wet a mouth that had suddenly gone dry. "You were just across the room."

Annoyance iced Gunda's tone. "He is a vampire, Gerwalta. Did you not understand that?"

The revelation should have made her more alert, but curiosity and amusement brought a smile to her face. "A vampire? In the Schwarzwald?" Then she recalled that she held a spear in her hand, its blade aimed for his heart, and allowed it to lower. "Apologies, but you are the first of your kind I have encountered in person… Spatar, was it?"

He grinned, taking her fingers in his hand and brushing a kiss against the back of her knuckles in the style of the laity courts. "The title is Romanian," he dropped her hand, "akin to your *Fürst*, I believe."

A prince? A prince of what? What kind of dark one held political office, and what would he be doing dining with the Red Matron?

"The Spatar comes all the way from Wallachia to extend a hand of friendship," the Matron said, refocusing their attention. With a wave of her hand, they sat. "He is an honored guest."

Gerwalta settled herself at the table, to the right of her mother, as the Spatar resumed his seat. "A friend is a most welcome thing indeed, Herr Spatar, though I do not think it required so long a journey."

The vampire's mouth cracked into an open smile. *No fangs.* Did not vampires have long canine teeth like the lupines? That's what she'd always heard. Did they shift into some other form as the wolves did?

"You were right about your daughter, Frau Matron," Karahan said. "Very observant. In truth, Fraulein," he turned back to her, "I have come via Ravensburg."

"Oh?" A stone dropped down Gerwalta's throat and settled into her stomach. "What business had you in Ravensburg, then?"

"I wished to hire a wolfsretter. One who could… eliminate the threat of a band of vampires causing some measure of disruption in the east."

At least he's not coming chasing the stories of what Andreas and I did in Nuremberg, then. The young wolfsretter lectured her manner, deparate not to show relief.

Gerwalta wove her fingers together and leaned over the table. "Is not this something a slayer would address? I was given to believe they balance your kind the way we do the lupines."

The vampire buried his frown behind a downward glance. "Verily, Fraulein, if I wished to kill the lot of them, that would be a wiser course of action. You are not a slayer; I cannot blame you for being unaware of the idiosyncrasies of vampires. You see, our natures prevent us from inducing the death of our own blooded-born. I do not know for certain if my asking a slayer to terminate my clutchson would, in fact, trigger my own death, but with seven involved, I need to be certain all are contained. Unfortunately, I do not have seven lives to give for the effort."

Gunda lowered her goblet. "Would not another bloodline would perform the deed for the right price?"

He clicked his tongue. "To do so would sow the seeds of a blood feud. No, Frau Matron, I am the author of this legacy, and I will write its final chapter the way I see best."

Her mother bobbed her head. "And we are somehow the quill you will use."

"As I cannot terminate my seven sons, I would have them contained. I wish for a wolfsretter to seal them in silver. I would then commit their care to you and your descendants."

"My descendants?" The wolfsretters exchanged furtive glances before Gunda continued. "How would you compensate my progeny?"

The vampire patted the corners of his mouth with a bit of cloth, though to the best of Gerwalta's recollection, he hadn't sampled a single thing on his plate. "What is it you wish, Frau Matron? Gold? Jewels? Land? I have all this and more and will give it gladly to see this task accomplished. I have a particularly fine estate just over the mountains to the south, on the edge of your dominion. If you wish it, it is yours."

Hunger narrowed Gunda's eyes. A Matron's power was drawn in part from the size of the region over which she reigned, and the amount of silver found therein. No doubt the Matron was considering now that the rich veins running through the southern regions of the Schwarzwald might also be found beyond the mountains. Not to mention, with four daughters at her disposal, having a new Vicematron to rule over an expanded territory would help secure its loyalty.

"That is fair payment," Gunda agreed, sitting back and drawing her goblet to her lips. "For the capture, that is. For the continued custodianship, I would ask something more."

Karahan dipped his head and opened his hands, palms up, on the table.

Gunda drank leisurely, set the goblet down, centered herself, and grinned. "You will owe me a blood debt."

For a creature who couldn't blush, the vampire's countenance boiled. Most mortal creatures would crumble under the fury of a vampire enraged. Gunda Faust was not *most* mortal creatures.

"How dare you!"

The Red Matron siphoned a bit of silver from a candlestick. The globule swam about her fingers, a tiny fish darting about on her whim. "You're asking me to send one of my warriors into harm's way and risk her life. To capture a single vampire? Perhaps that would merit the estate alone. But seven? I should ask for *seven* blood debts in kind, but I will settle for one. I believe the offer quite generous."

Karahan grew small in his chair. "Fine, it is agreed, though…" His hand shot forward, one long finger extended. "…do not fool yourself for a moment that this is a good thing. You marry the fate of my bloodline and yours, there's no telling what the consequences may be."

If there was one fault for which Gunda Faust could be tacked, it was her inability to see fate beyond her own grave. "As it will be, let it be so. We have a deal, then. You have disposal of Gerwalta." The Matron raised her hand in indication. "She recently proved herself a credit to my bloodline in a matter outside the Schwarzwald."

Karahan dipped his head in Gerwalta's direction. "Fraulein Faust, I will see to your provisions. What is it you will require?"

It was the Matron, however, who answered. "She needs only be pointed a direction, and to have silver at her side. To contain seven undead, some significant portion of it. Can you arrange its safe transport?"

"Of course." The vampire looked insulted by the very instigation it could be otherwise.

Gerwalta roused herself, bowing to both mother and guest. "I will see to my affairs, then. Mother, the ball?"

"Shall be delayed until such time as your return," Gunda said. "Though do make haste. I will tolerate the House of Night in my dominion, but no longer than is necessary."

She wanted to ask her mother why she'd invite the only bloodline that rivaled their own to compete for her hand if she found them so distasteful, but how could she with an outsider amongst them?

The young warrior bowed to acknowledge the order before turning on Karahan. "If I can ask, Herr Spatar, where is it we are traveling to? I may have need of different attire depending."

"Of course, Fraulein. We are bound for Venice. I will bid you good evening and prepare my own for departure. Meet me in the village at sundown."

There truly was a god. Such a trip would take weeks, months perhaps. Even dark ones could not cover such a large distance in less than a fortnight. Another month, at least, of remaining unbound to a husband. If only it could be forever.

"Very well. Until tomorrow, then."

A pink and amber sky served as backdrop as Gerwalta walked through the south gates, carrying only her cloak, the clothing she wore, a measure of concealed silver, and a smidgen of gold with her. Food could be bartered or hunted. Weapons forged with her power. Water was all about on the ground in the form of snow. Her boots were wearing thin, but there was no time to have a new pair made. Besides, no other could equal the comfort. The peasant boy Andreas hired to break them in last year had been truly inspired to place them on a cow for a day. Not all laymen ideas were poor ones.

Half way down the mountain, the world turned upside down.

A flash of red, a swish of flaxen hair, and suddenly, a silver-studded staff pressed into Gerwalta's sternum, pinning her to the ground.

"Do not think I do not see what you are after, little sister."

"Helga?" Gerwalta gasped. "I… do not…"

"Silence!"

Bright lights flooded her vision as the butt of Helga's weapon met her temple. As the weight lifted, her body instinctively curled into a ball, fearing further onslaught. Slowly at first, then suddenly, her eyes regained focus, the fleeting light of day a salve to the pain.

"Do you not think I understand what you're about," her sister said. "First *exposing* the Dregers, now convincing mother to let you play party to some rich and powerful vampire's ploys. I'll credit you with this sister: your professed disinterest in leadership blinded me to how well you were plotting to obtain it."

"I *am* disinterested." Gerwalta rolled over on all fours, lecturing herself not to evidence her torment. "Everyone knows that you'll be next Matron, and that includes me. I am only carrying out the task our mother has set before me as a dutiful daughter."

"Did the Matron command you to *execute* Bernhard?" A few feet away, Helga held her bostaff at the ready, prepared to strike if Gerwalta counterattacked. "Surely you must have known how impressed our mother would be by your ability to slay the very man you were to wed."

Summoning every ounce of determination, Gerwalta pushed herself to her feet without wincing. "You misunderstand, sister. Bernhard's death was self-defense; I am owed no glory for that kill. Nor should you envy my assignment to this task. I am being sent to capture seven vampires. *Seven!* Even you must know how dangerous such a deed is. I was selected not because it is an opportunity to prove my worth, but because I am as I ever was: an expendable asset."

She'd only meant to present a rationalization, but it amazed Gerwalta how the words hung heavy with truth.

Helga retracted first her weapon, then her person, making no attempt at amends or reconciliation. Instead, she turned, pausing to add over her shoulder, "When I am Matron, little sister, that will be no less true," before she disappeared back into the forest.

THREE

This time when he sensed one of their kind approaching the hamlet, Andreas did not wonder over which came. He scented her on the wind.

Only, why was she here?

"Herr Konigswolf?" She drew to a stop when she caught his eyes in the square. "What are you doing here?"

"I am here because…" he said sheepishly before regaining his confidence. Was he not a king? Why did he cower before her? "Well, because, I am leaving Triberg, of course."

Her face went white. "What?"

"Temporarily," Andreas quickly amended. The smile she tried to hide warmed him. Not so different after all, was she? "Walta, how do you—"

"Ah, Herr Baron!"

They both turned to find Spatar Karahan, his arms filled with three casks, walking their direction.

"And Fraulein Faust." He gave both a friendly nod as he passed. "Good to see you both. We're all here then and ready to go, I presume?"

Her jaw dropped. Ah, so she was not aware of his involvement. Curious, as hers was the only reason he'd agreed to the journey. But if not for him, *why* was she here?

Gerwalta turned on him. "Explain."

"You first."

"I am under contract to Spatar Karahan on behalf of the House of Red."

"A contract to what?"

"*That* is none of your concern."

He stepped closer. "A marriage contract?"

"What?" Her face screwed up. "Of course not. Why would I wed a... *foreigner?*"

Her quick substitution protected the truth from a passing layman who looked at them both with utter confusion. It was not that wolfsretter and lupines never came into the village, it was that it was never together. She did not resist when he took her by the arm and dragged her to a space between two buildings, hidden from public view.

"What are you doing? Get your hands off me. I *will* silver you."

"No, you won't." He spun her about. "The truth now, Walta, what is the nature of this contract?"

"To use silver to trap a few renegade vampires, if you insist to know." Her hand flattened against his chest, shoving him. "Which does not require the aid of a lupine, so go home."

"I will not. I *cannot.*"

"And why is that, precisely?"

"Because I volunteered myself to be your bodyguard."

Her eyes went wide. "Why would *I* need a bodyguard?"

"I assumed it was some sort of trickery, a means to disguise my purpose at your instruction. The moment when Karahan said he needed a wolf to help protect Fraulein Gerwalta Faust, I volunteered."

She huffed and tried to walk past him. "I will speak to Karahan to resolve this. Leave, Andreas. I do not want you here."

He took her by the arm, pulling her flush to him. The heat between them? It kindled without need for flame. "Where do you want me, Walta?"

Gerwalta turned her eyes away. "Please, do not distract me with attempts at lovemaking."

"You think I merely *attempt*, good woman? Mark my words, when I am successful, you will not mind so being *distracted*. And nothing you can say will stop me from coming. If you think I'm going to let you wander off without my protection, whether you will it or no, you clearly don't understand my commitment to your good fortune."

From blushed to blanched in a moment, she conjured her cloak, a reminder that the piece of cloth he'd have to go through to find her heart was more than merely physical. It wrapped about her soul with the same tenacity with which it fell upon her shoulders.

The wolf's head cocked to the side. "It marvels me each time you do that. Is it always red? Why a riding cloak? You don't even ride."

"Yes, it's always red. That is my dominant bloodline and all I can conjure. And a riding cloak? I don't know. I suppose because that's what my family does. Other bloodlines manifest their cloaks in different…" She cut herself off. "Why are we discussing this?"

"Because that's what two people in love do, they endeavor to learn about each other."

The wolfsretter rolled her eyes. "Why do you endure with this fantasy? Do you think this is some tale of old, and we are two destined lovers brought together by fate?"

His brow furrowed. "Of course, not. There's no such thing as fate."

Gerwalta threw her hands up in the air. "Fine, come then, but if you think you're going to make love to me all the way to Venice, you have another thing coming."

The weight of what was being asked took on the form of a lodestone in his stomach. "Venice? But it's…"

Thronged by people. Barren of forest. Surrounded by water.

Ruled by vampires.

She grinned. "Did you not know that part?"

"Our discussions never progressed that far."

She finally managed to skirt around him. "I know how much you hate crowded places, Andreas. Nuremberg is nothing compared to Venice. Travelers have brought us tales: they say the city folds in on itself like a cake. People, buildings, and more people."

He cleared his throat, regaining his resolution. "More the

reason for me to accompany you. I will brave all to protect you. It is my duty as your future mate."

Gerwalta's eyes rolled in full measure as she turned away. "Lord protect me from delusional wolves and besotted men, and most of all, from those who are both."

"And the silver?"

Gerwalta looked up from the manifest Spatar Karahan had provided upon her arrival for examination. *In case she wished to add to it before leaving,* he said. These vampires and their preoccupation with material things. Why did he not understand that her kind needed little? The only thing she did need, however, she did not see listed.

The vampire demurred. "No need to be concerned; I have made arrangements. Venice will be ready for us when we arrive. In the meantime, I trust you have enough for the journey?"

Her hands instinctively went to her abdomen, rubbing the plates concealed on her person. Until they arrived at Venice, there wasn't need to mount any defense; they had no enemy on the road save the occasional, itinerant highway men. Surely between a vampire lord, a fourth-daughter wolfsretter, and a konigswolf, they could muster enough force to deter such efforts.

She bobbed her head as Karahan's footman, an enlightened layman by the name of Francisco, brushed passed, buckets of water for each of the horses swinging from his stubby arms. "Indeed."

The Spatar scanned the moonlit village roads. "We should depart to make as good a measure before sunrise. Where is Herr Baron? He has not changed his mind, has he?"

If only. "No, he is there," she vaguely motioned to the very alcove in which they'd had their tete-a-tete. "Waiting. Observing."

Annoying.

The vampire drew in a deep breath and then, leaning forward, squinted his eyes. "Are you certain? I can make out no sign of him."

"Spatar Karahan, Andreas Baron is a konigswolf. Do not assume that you have any hope of seeing him when he does not wish to be seen. He could stalk a rabbit in the desert without detection. He will make himself known when the need arises."

And it must have arisen now, for as soon as the words slipped out, Andreas rounded the corner and strode into the square. Now that the anger had subsided, and she could take him in at large instead of a hand's length from her face, she observed him at leisure. Thus, the surprise.

Andreas's garb may still be that of a farmer, but it was by far the finest frock a farmer could have. The deep blue waistcoat boasted brocade, even if a simple loop. It fit him tightly from shoulder to waist, though tapered somewhat after that over a pair of brown breeches that did not have a single remade stich or bit of fray. The baggy coat over and white shirt under appeared freshly laundered, or perhaps, never worn. The only bit of his person she did recognize from previous interactions were Andreas's boots: well-worn animal hide, easily pulled off in case the need for taking one's fur arose.

He made a slight bow of his head when he reached them. "My apologies for keeping you waiting."

For this vision, she'd have waited for the saints to rise from their graves. Gerwalta motioned to the vampire standing to the right.

Karahan clapped his hands. "Good. I shall ride inside—"The vampire pointed to the coach behind them. "—there. I would suppose that both of you prefer to go on, ped-a-ped?"

Andreas looked to Gerwalta for guidance. The wolf nodded. "Yes, I believe that is best."

"Wonderful." Karahan proceeded to open the passenger compartment door. "If we keep good pace and are graced with good weather, we should be able to make Venice just in time, three weeks from now. It would be quicker in summer, if we should be able to cross the Alps, but it is winter now and the roads over the mountains are closed."

A chill ran down her spine. Two weeks with Andreas. Two more back. Their previous endeavor had barely been more than a fortnight, and it still proved enough time for them to fall in love. Where would a month and then some leave them?

"Fraulein Faust, I trust you have a proper gown to appear at the court of the Doge when we arrive to Venice?"

Her eyes went wide. "You said nothing about visiting vampire royalty."

Karahan sneered. "An assumption on my part that you would expect it. No mind. If you have nothing, Messer Mazzi can provide."

Mazzi? Who was Mazzi?

She looked at herself, then to the wolf grinning sheepishly beside her. "What about him?"

The Spatar gave the konigswolf an assessing look. "If you're able to keep your present wear in such condition, Herr Baron, I believe it would be wholly suitable. By the by, if I can say, it is a fetching waistcoat."

"Thank you, Spatar." Andreas bent at the waist to acknowledge the compliment as Karahan moved to open the coach door.

Flabbergasted, Gerwalta turned a flack jaw on the wolf who offered her hand of assistance. Then, squaring herself, she drew up and away from the wolf with haste, landing on the front bench in a brew of annoyance.

FOUR

Three days out of Triberg, they passed into lands outside Gunda Faust's control.

Gerwalta circled her shoulders as though trying to work away the anxiety of leaving her clan's region for the first time. "I need to run."

Andreas, walking on wordlessly for some time, began to take off his overcoat. "I will accompany you."

"I would prefer to be alone."

"Did not we discuss this last time we traveled? In the land of the laity, proper young women do not strut unaccompanied through forest in the middle of the night. It is unlikely you'd encounter anyone at this hour, but this is still a laymen road. Perhaps ahead there are travelers who've stopped to make camp for the night."

"I have no intention of adapting the feigning nature of lay women simple to avoid judgment by those whose opinion means less than nothing."

Andreas bristled. "And what of my opinion?"

Gerwalta gave him a fleeting burn of her eyes before they silvered over the moment she pulled her cloak into being. With that, she was off, leaving Andreas's questions unanswered.

The werewolf heard a chuckle to his left and turned to find the vampire watching from an open window of his coach, amusement barely concealed.

"And you?" Andreas asked. "Do you think it proper, her being about all alone?"

"Oh, dear Herr Baron. If a layman meets *her* on the path and assumes any liberties, I fear he'd not live to see the sunrise."

Andreas grimaced. "I see you will be no help."

"Not in the way you're hoping, no. But do carry on. I find your behavior around each other highly entertaining. When one grows so old in years as I have, such amusements are fewer and far between."

Gerwalta had not gotten too far down the road when his scent carried upon the breeze. *Damned, persistent wolf.* She spun, manifesting silver claws over the tips of her leather riding gloves.

Andreas paused, smirking. "Are you a cat now, Walta?"

He used her silence to close the distance between them, taking one of her hands in his, gingerly rubbing the back of her gloves while avoiding contact with the metal. "It is a bad ploy. Recall that dogs chase cats."

Before he succeeded at drawing her hand to his lips, she pulled back, rounded, and continued her way up the road. "Cease! You know your efforts can come to naught."

"What do you mean, to naught?" He kept apace, though with his relaxed manner, his hands laced behind his back, she'd have thought him strolling an avenue instead of shuffling at a wolfsretter's speed. "By my reckoning, we will be away from the trappings of our familial duties for at least a month. We should make use of the time."

"But we will go home again, will we not?" she said. "And all the issues that kept us apart before will be waiting, with interest. Dismiss this lackadaisical fantasy you've concocted that there is a path for us to be together. I assure you, there is not one that does not end with your death."

"I know this. I *understand* it, even."

She stopped, spun. "And yet you endure?"

He stepped into her space, bringing them chest to chest. "I cannot stop. I have fallen in love with you, and not to honor the desire of my heart is its own kind of death. If I am to choose between the two, I will fight for the one wherein you call out your pleasure beneath me."

She would *not* give him the benefit of knowing how those words sent a pulse of anticipation through her body.

Though the way the corner of his mouth twitched, she

suspected he knew.

Damn wolves!

She turned, increasing her pace. "Consign yourself to a lifetime of unrequited love should you wish. I, however, am getting married."

Sweeping feet, he circled on her, walking backward. "Tell yourself that, my lamb. Oh, your mother may march you out like livestock in the market. You may even become betrothed, but you'll never find a lover in your bed."

Her face boiled. "Stop discussing anything in the area of my bed! We will never be together, least of all in bed."

"It may be the floor. Or the ground, even. We are both dark ones; there is no need for us to carry on as the laity do."

The silver kissed his throat as she struck, drawing a droplet of blood to the dagger's edge. His eyes showed no fear, but his tongue finally stilled.

"You are determined to forget your own nature, Andreas, do *not* presume I will do the same. I am a wolfsretter, I am your superior, your dominant. If you insist on taking advantage of a momentary weakness on my part a year ago——"

"It was hardly momentary, pet."

Her fingernail bit deeper, drawing a gasp from the king. "*If* you insist, then I am well within my rights to end you."

Their eyes became the bridge of their tensions. The skin beneath her silver smoked, hissed, poisoned him, but Andreas's stare had the same effect on Gerwalta.

Karahan emerged from the coach which had come to rest on the road behind them. "Why have we stopped?"

Francisco coughed, his German true but heavily-accented with foreign flavor. "I believe the woman's about to kill the man, sir. Didn't want to miss it, I'm not likely to see a fair thing like her get the best of something his size again."

Karahan's brow furrowed before his form dissolved, becoming smoke. The cloud of his being funneled through the air, before assuming a corporeal form just a few feet from standoff. He snatched up

Gerwalta's hand with the speed of lightning.

"With all respects to you and your prerogatives, I must insist that until the terms of our contract are fulfilled, you not set about destroying each other," the vampire lectured, snapping each from the showdown. He lowered Gerwalta's hand to her side by force. "Put aside this transgression, whatever its cause, until you are on your own time and ground again."

The vampire, seemingly satisfied that the storm had passed, meandered away. "You may resume passive-aggressively charming each other at will."

Her disgust took the physical form of a curled lip as she turned on Andreas. "You *are* insane."

"No, Fraulein." The Spatar squeezed the konigwolf's shoulder. "He is in love. Men in love do crazy things, but that does not make him crazy."

Andreas blinked. "But you will pay me then?"

"Yes, Herr Baron. I may have taken advantage of your zeal, but I will not exploit your time."

"All men are fools." She spun on heel, huffing. "Venice grows no closer by the flapping of lips in lieu of the actions of our feet. Hurry, so that we can be all the faster to leave it."

FIVE

The German tongue found no friend where they stopped to rest or resupply. Gerwalta's French gave her three more nights of utility, but beyond that, even it became scarce.

Dawn tickled the horizon of the twelfth dawn, their camp made as usual on the side of the road, when Gerwalta awoke to the feeling of fur on her fingers. The wolf licked her gloveless hands. In between sleep and waking, she pushed away the nudging snout before closing her eyes again. She let the lazy web of sleep pull her back down, entirely at ease.

"Gerwalta, wake up."

Her body shook. She opened her eyes again, this time to see the man, not the wolf. Dead leaves clung to the curls of his chestnut hair, the unkempt mass of it wet with dew.

And he was, as wolves had the aggravating habit of being, completely nude.

She closed her eyes again, though this time from propriety instead of fatigue. "Do put on something before you rouse me from sleep."

"I'll not indulge your attempts at modesty. You know full well what my naked form looks like, and I have no shame wearing it. Even if I were not in love with you, I am a lupine and this is our way."

"And what of Francisco? He is a layman and a devout Catholic. Seeing a naked man might send him into hysterics, or worse, confession."

The wolf grimaced. "It matters not. They are both gone."

That succeeded in bringing her to her feet, her cloak-turned-coverlet falling to the ground.

Gerwalta worked her boots on to her feet. "The coach?"

"Also gone. And that's not all." The king-wolf's head turned toward the nearby road. "There is a scent of lupine on the wind."

Gerwalta reached to her belting, pulling the two custom-carved wooden hilts she'd commissioned after her last trip with Andreas. She'd learned not to assume appropriate bases for her weapons would always be found just lying about the forest floor. In a wink, her silver reserves obeyed, pulling long and filling into thin, eager blades the length of her forearm.

"To the best of my knowledge, there are no packs in this area. Why would there be a lupine here?"

"Just because I am one does not mean I can explain the actions of all. Each lupine is his own man, driven by his own needs and desires."

"Save me the philosophy lessons, Andreas." She pointed to the deeper forest. "Lead us. You are a better tracker than me."

"That must have cost you some pride to admit."

"Pride is too high a cost for denying the truth, and often turns deadly if done with haste."

"Who is philosophizing now?"

"Andreas!"

Without further retort, the konigswolf took his fur. Gerwalta took to the trees, though winter had left the branches bare and her red cloak made for easy placement against the brown and black of sleeping oaks. To her surprise, he led her not into the thicket where a lupine was more likely to be found, but directly up the road. A quarter hour had passed when Andreas came to a sudden holt, his body tense. His massive head swung right, swung left, swung right again, before his deep brown eyes searched for her in the canopy.

"What is it?"

A high whine lifted on the air. Gerwalta used each of her senses, trying to discern what had Andreas in such a quandary. Neither sight nor sound nor scent informed.

Until the arrow pierced her shoulder.

The earth would hit her hard, but that wasn't what concerned her as she fell. What did was a wolf of golden pelt who'd just emerged from behind a row of boulders, looking intent on causing the injury the fall would not.

She landed with a thud but knew her survival depended upon ignoring the pain. Andreas howled, tickling her defenses, rousing her instincts. The golden wolf leapt, attempting to clamp his massive jaws, but the wolfsretter managed to arrest her descent and throw herself backward and out of the way. By the time she was on two feet, she had her blade in hand.

The golden wolf rounded, teeth exposed, a growl in his throat.

Gerwalta readied herself, leaning back on her stronger foot, preparing to lunge. "Come along, then, wolfie. Taste my silver."

But no sooner had it sprung than a blur of red and brown fur whisked across her vision. Andreas bit, the golden howled, growled, countered. Fur flew, as did blood, all the time the pain on Gerwalta's shoulder peaking with each move she made. What to do? Her strength, her precision? Her injury compromised both. If she dove in between them, attempting to strike, she'd be just as likely to hit Andreas as the attacking golden.

And then she spotted it: the coach, sitting just off the road, somewhat obscured behind a bank of stout firs. Even the Spatar's two horses were reigned properly, waiting to proceed if only given the command. Was the vampire still secured inside? What of his human?

The tide of the battle of wolves had begun to shift, Andreas's victory all but assured once the smaller lupine he was fighting accepted he'd been beaten. Gerwalta, then, crossed to the trussed-up kit and knocked on the door.

"Spatar Karahan. Are you in there?"

Would he hear her? *Could* he hear her? It suddenly occurred to Gerwalta that she knew very little of the nature of vampires, something she best remedy if she was expected to face one down, let alone seven.

She pressed her ear to the door. They weren't in direct sunlight here amidst the trees, but did that matter?

Finally, when she'd just about convinced herself that she *needed* to open the door to be certain, a voice called out.

"Yes, I am fine."

Gerwalta let out a halted breath. "And Francisco?"

The voice was softer this time. "He is… in *here* with me."

Gerwalta's face screwed up. "Why would he be in…"

Abruptly, she cut off her own words instead of laying down evidence of her ignorance.

"Very well," she amended, spinning around as sounds of conflict rose anew. "Stay in there safe, the both of you, until I retrieve you. There is trouble afoot, but nothing Andreas and I cannot handle."

Back in the fray, she found the wolves engaged. Andreas could defeat him; she knew he could. But for some reason he showed restraint. He wasn't going to allow their attacker to walk away, was he? Though a lupine, he must know the fallacy of disengaging with honor in a conflict which had none.

Nothing else to be done except what must be. She withdrew the silver, gathering it in her hands, forcing it to spin out long and thin. The cord did not need to be extensive; a single loop would do. She made it so, then used the distraction of their continued battle to gain distance. Andreas caught sight of her only as he leapt, throwing herself on the back of the beast trying to kill him.

The silver loop tightened, finding skin beneath fur. In an instant, the lupine howled in pain.

They were far from the Schwarzwald where German was the tongue of kings, but what else could she do? "Who are you? Why are you trying to kill us?"

"Don't bother asking. I know who he is." Andreas followed suit, shedding fur and standing on two feet beside her. "His name is Gerhart Hessian, and he is of the Wehr Pack."

"The Wehr Pack? But we passed through their territory days ago. What would he be doing this far from his packlands?"

"What, indeed." The konigswolf nodded. "Remove his binding so he may lose his fur. Give him a chance to tell us."

Furtive eyes looked to the wolf to get his visual assurance that the situation was well in paw. Andreas caught her eyes, the unspoken promise palpable in the air. *I won't let him hurt you.*

The wolfsretter turned back to the captive lupine who, despite the pain evident in his eyes, kept his teeth bared. One deep breath of moist, winter air, and with her exhale, the silver liquified, flowing in rivulets back up her arms.

Andreas descended, his massive biceps and thick thighs working under taut skin. The konigswolf was fearsome as an animal, but even as a man, he fell upon the beast before them, forcing him to submission.

"Take your skin, rapscallion!" Andreas demanded, pushing the creature's maw into the mud. "I will have the truth from your tongue, or I swear, I will send you home to your king without it."

The gray wolf flexed, trying with one desperate huff to break free, until the fight fled from his eyes. His body eased with a whimper, his chest cycling a breath as he began to shift under Andreas's hold.

"There you are." The king-wolf scowled. "Now, out with it. Why are you after the vampire?"

"Vampire?" Gerhart asked, wincing as Andreas shifted atop him, pressing down on the pressure points most effective for a man. "Why would I be after a vampire?"

Gerwalta blinked. "But you were trying to make off with coach."

"The coach?" The lupine became partner to her confusion. "I didn't touch the coach. It was that layman who's with you who did. I watched him."

Andreas and she exchanged a look.

"Why would Francisco move the coach away from us?"

"I do not know." Gerwalta scanned the nearby forest. "Possibly, to assure privacy."

"Privacy?" The konigswolf repeated. "Privacy for what purpose?"

She didn't know how to properly convey meaning without implication, so instead, she just made some vague gesticulations with her hands, adding after, "As I understand it."

"Oh?" The lines in Andrea's forehead flattened as his brow lifted, his eyes going wide. "Oh, I see." He cleared his throat. "Well then, Gerhart. If you weren't after Karahan, you were after us. Why?"

"Because my king commanded it."

Andrea's brow furrowed. "What cause would Michael have to bare fang against me? He and I have no quarrel."

"I cannot, nor would I, presume to know the workings of my king's mind."

The way Gerhart's king conducted the leadership must be different from how Andreas went about it, Gerwalta thought. Whatever bias her siblings held against lupines inherently, not even Helga would disagree that Andreas governed through diplomacy and open dialog, not brute force or unclear ultimatums. There seemed to be some wager among her older sisters about when such a strategy would fall under the weight of its own fantasy.

Gerwalta wracked what she knew of the Wehr pack from her brain. It was a collection of about two dozen lupines whose packlands lay on the southern reaches of Red territory. She herself had never interacted with any of them, but her mother had, and very recently.

Helga.

"Gerwalta?"

The concern in Andreas's voice anchored into her thoughts and pulled them back to the present. Gerwalta blinked away her confusion, wondering if it had been moments or minutes that she'd been lost to world. It was funny how a stark realization could do that, create a wake of time that distorted understanding.

"It was my sister."

"Which one?"

"Helga. She… She thinks I am threatening her claim on the matronship. How convenient would it be if I met a tragic death outside the jurisdiction of the House of Red. Helga ordered the Wehr konigswolf to see to me murdered."

Andreas turned his attention back on Gerhart, forcing his hand behind his back, twisting his wrist to induce a bite of pain. "Is that the way of it?"

Gerhart squealed. "How do I know? But if you were any kind of self-respecting konigswolf, you'd kill her yourself rather than curl up to her when you sleep each day."

A wave of nerves ran through her. Curl up to her? Andreas slept some distance from her each morning. Did he not?

Even if that wasn't the case, the larger issue was plain: Gerhart had been ordered to kill her by his king, and she knew nothing but death or the revocation of the order would keep him from carrying out the command. Without further word, Gerwalta drew the silver cord in, collapsing it into a broad-edged dagger. She readied a lethal blow before Andreas caught her arm from the air.

"Gerwalta, wait!"

Frustration fueled her anger. "For what? You heard what he said!"

"Precisely. He is acting of compulsion, not his own conscious. *He* is innocent."

"Do you suppose his disdain for me would be lessened if he was acting of his own regard?"

On that stark truth, the konigswolf's eyes twitched, before his face became somber. "Even so, it would not be deserving of death. If all wolfsretters and lupines slaughtered each other based on emotions alone, we'd all be dead."

She softened around the edges. "I have no desire for his blood, Andreas, but only his own end will keep him from carrying out the deed. His king has commanded it, and it is obligation."

"I agree."

That stopped her quicker than did his grip. "You agree, then, that I need kill him?"

Andreas pushed her weapon hand to her side, "No. I mean that I agree that under his king's command, he will not stray. However, there is another way."

"Another way?" Her knowledge did not suggest anything but that one of them must die. "What?"

"If he pledges his fealty to me now and becomes of my pack, I can divert that command."

What the devil? "You'd invite an enemy to harbor under your maw?"

"He is *not* an enemy. Why can you not understand that?"

"Because I don't understand wanting to show mercy to my would-be killer."

"Love her?" Gerhart piped up. His rusty gaze turned on the king. "You… You… betrayer!"

Andreas huffed his frustration. "And now the mirror shows its reflection."

As Gerhart struggled, trying one last time to wriggle out from Andreas's hold, the wolf king picked up the captive's hands before smashing both back over his head. Gerwalta heard the bones crack.

Andreas did not stall. "Just because I make you pack does not mean I have to like you, Gerhart. And I don't. But I'd rather hate your hide than see it made into a wolfsretter's rug. Submit to me, and I will remove this burden to your soul."

"And serve my days as pup to a king whose betrayed his kind? No, thank you."

Gerwalta drew her blade high in the air. "My way, then."

"No!" Terror pulled the color from Gerhart's face. "Fine. I submit! I accept you as my king, I pledge my fealty. I pledge my life!"

Gerwalta panicked as both wolves grew still, moments before Andreas threw his head back. Despite his layman form, the konigswolf managed a howl, a deep, crisp wail, joined a moment later by this lupine struggling beneath him. A quickening. She'd heard stories of it, read accounts, but the sacred act was rarely witnessed by one of her kind.

Andreas had barely stood when his balance faltered. Gerwalta maneuvered beneath him, keeping him from the ground. A moment passed that way before he began to find his footing again. She'd credit him this time with not taking advantage of circumstance, making no crude implication or suggestive quip. What he did do, however, was much worse. With aching tenderness, the konigswolf reached a hand to her chin and pulled her eyes to his, smiling.

And then, he was back on his feet and walking away, leaving her insides wobbling.

Damn wolf.

"Go to Triberg," Andreas ordered his new packling. "Find Wilhelm and ask him to assign you a place to bed down and a share of work. You are now forbidden to kill any wolfsretter."

"And do not tell anyone that Andreas loves me," Gerwalta rushed to add.

Andreas's face cycled from annoyance to understanding. "And tell no one of our relationship," he acquiesced before turning to Gerwalta and adding, "But at some point, it will become known, and as soon as you admit it, we will need to discuss how to handle that discovery."

She let him fall to the ground. "You really are quite frustrating."

Gerhart grinned when he and his new king sat eye-to-eye on the ground. "Is this the pack I've agreed to join to save my life, one where the king moons over a matron's bitch? I might be tempted to reconsider my pledge of fealty."

"Gerwalta will be happy to separate your head from your body, if you like."

His new packling shuddered. "At least this one loves you, though a nose full of snot that will do for you."

The Wehr pack could benefit from a lesson in manners. Andreas swept his hand across the air. "Off now. When I return, we will become better-acquainted."

"And her?" Gerhart nodded at Gerwalta.

Andreas bobbed his head. "If she lasts the week without admitting her feelings, then I'll be a pup's first fang."

SIX

Andreas's head rested on her lap as his body rose and fell with the gentle waves of slumber. Given that he'd saved her life, she couldn't find the will to push him away when he'd rolled near her by the fire, finishing out their day sleep stretched atop her red cloak.

The konigswolf had been so overtaxed by the quickening, he'd not bothered to pull back on his breeches. Gerwalta would like to say that her eyes had not taken advantage of the unobstructed view. It wasn't as if she'd never seen a naked lupine before. Not even as if she'd never seen *Andreas* nude. But that did not mean she'd had opportunity to examine at length… well, his *length*.

Truth be told, she found the actual *implement* rather unimpressive. It was a funny looking thing, like a toadstool that had barely managed to peek out from a patch of loose soil. She couldn't understand, therefore, why her sisters seemed so enamored of their encounters with their husbands. Perhaps a lupine's asset was different? For all she knew, perhaps the whole procedure with them was different. They were half-animal, after all. Surely that must have consequences in the realm of intimacy.

She knew the basics of the marital bed, at least the mechanics of it, to say. Would that tiny thing even be big enough to go inside? Gerwalta closed her eyes and tried to imagine it, but the vision was more comical than tempting. But the moment she imagined herself straddled over him, bending down to taste his kiss, and his hands rising to cup her breasts, the last thing it was, was comical.

It wasn't until Andreas's lips pursed against her fingertips that she realized she'd been tracking the contours of his mouth.

His grin broadened into a smile. "What are you thinking of, love, that has caused such a change in your scent?"

It had taken several moments for Andreas to realize the tickle on his lips was not part of the dream in which he'd been enveloped. It was better, for it was truly happening.

Only a king's ransom of self-restraint kept him still for so long. He knew Gerwalta would not undertake such affections whilst he was awake. Not yet, anyhow. But he'd seen her feigned annoyance and indifference begin to fade these last few days. She had stopped calling him *Herr Baron* or *Herr Konigswolf,* regressing to Andreas. When he deftly neared her while sleeping in the day, she no longer unconsciously pulled in on herself. After the previous excitement, it had been *she* who offered *him* a share of her cloak-turned-bed to stay off the frosted forest floor.

He let her fingertips indulge in their exploration for as long as he could, wondering if she would make further endeavors to explore boldly. Her movement slowed, the pressure amplified, her heartbeat ticked up and her breathing deepened. And then came the change in her scent. He remembered it from one of their previous encounters, the distinct mix of pine and cold air and feminine hue that signaled her arousal.

After that, how could he possibly stay still?

"What are you thinking of, love, that has caused your eyes to silver over?"

Like the children's tales of old, the waking moment spoiled the spell.

Gerwalta's hand retracted. "I have no idea what you mean."

No, she would not dismiss it with such a casual denial.

The wolfsretter yelped as he turned over and hefted himself on all fours, crawling over her with such speed, it made her dizzy. "Your mouth is too pretty for lies, my pet."

She fell on to her back, for there was no where else to go. His weight settled atop her in the most delicious way, and finally, she did not fight him. In fact, one of her legs hitched up, buckling his hip, bringing them into better alignment. It may the preamble to a defensive move, but if so, she was delaying its execution for some reason.

"Fine," Gerwalta huffed. "Allow me to rephrase: it *means* nothing."

"What doesn't?"

"That I find you attractive. You are handsome, and you are nude. And I am… of an age to appreciate such things for their own merit without the complication."

"So, all you desire is my body, not the heart within it?" His mouth descended to her neck. He could dig the well before collecting the water if she wished. "You do not think that dissuades me, do you? There is a reason it's called 'making love,' Gerwalta. The physical act kindles the emotions beneath it."

"There are no emotions beneath it. I respect you, perhaps I still even like you, but that is all. I am quite sure what you're implying requires marriage."

"You don't need a husband." Another roll, and her body did the most amazing thing: it rolled back. His hands traipsed down her sides, anchoring around her lower back. This time, her other leg rose, and she folded her ankles behind his back. Sweet mercy, if not for the cloth of her breeches, he'd be inside her. His body recognized the proximity, drove him to mimic the act as though they were nude. Gerwalta's hands embraced him, pulled him closer. Her nails raked into his back.

The heat where they were nearly joined… he could feel it. Feel her tensions building. Feel her desires pooling.

"It will be…" She swallowed hard; a guttural noise that made him increase his pace. "…difficult to wed without one."

"You're not going to be wed." Roll. Counterroll. Dear Lord, she was undoing him. Was she, too, as close to the edge as he? He did hope, for he wasn't sure how much longer his restraint or her passion would at last.

"You're going to be…"

Push. Pull. He lifted one arm as his other reached under her hip, pulling her hard into him as he gave another roll.

"…*mine*."

"I will n——nah——*ahh*."

Gerwalta's head lolled back, her chest heaving with breath. Her nails pierced his skin. Andreas didn't care. She was climaxing from his touch, riding pleasure from his actions. She could have half the blood in his body if she wanted it.

She could have his *anything*.

Which pushed him to say the worst possible thing. "Gerwalta, I love you. Let me mate you now, here. Let me make love to—"

In a heartbeat, it was over.

Gerwalta flipped him with ease, reversing their positions. Andreas grinned as the wolfsretter straddled him, her arms pinning his back over his head. Until he saw the look on her face, that was.

Anger flared in her cheeks. "Do you really think you'll just mate me and be damned with my needs? My wants? My expectations?"

Had she just tacitly acknowledged the prospect? *Stay focused.* "You want me. Do not deny it: I can taste your desire in the air."

"Just because you will be bonded to me when we make love does not mean I will be to you."

His smile lit the forest. "*When?*"

"If!" she rushed to amend. "I am not a lupine. A wolfsretter expects to be courted. There are formalities, customs..."

Why was she telling him this? Did she want him better educated on how to woo her? He was eager for the instruction.

Andreas tried to lift his lips to hers, but her dominance prevented it. He found himself a hand's breadth from her mouth, his gaze lingering on her lips. "Name it and it shall be done."

"You must learn to dance."

He blinked thrice. "Sorry, what?"

"Court dances," Gerwalta said. "And I fear the motions are a little more complex than *this*."

She rolled her hips only meaning it as mockery but cursed the beautiful friction the movement induced.

Andreas threw back his head and bit his lips. "Mercy, Gerwalta. If you wish for me not to make love to you, mercy. I am already on the edge of arrival."

Now she blinked. "Arrival?"

"Yes, love, what just happened to you… *almost* happened to you, it will happen to me too."

"Do you think me a fool, Herr Konigswolf? I am not some little shewolf unwise to the ways of men and women. Just because I have not done the deed myself does it mean I am ignorant of the process. Remember that I have three older sisters, and Lord help me, an older brother who does not think our corridor of the castle has an echo."

It had not been his intent to insult her, but he'd managed the feat, nonetheless. *Curses.* He had to be cautious. Gerwalta's walls were beginning to fall, but if he pulled too fast, he'd be crushed under the wreckage. He could see that now. He'd gone after her like she was a wolf, but as she herself had reminded him, that was hardly true. If he wanted her as a mate, he'd need to also pursue her on her terms.

He doused his desire and fell back, pushing his laced hands behind his head. "Do you propose to teach me these dances? These courting rituals of your kind?"

"Yes, though not so that you may court me, but because my sisters and mother are all anticipating your ignorance of such things at the ball. They mean to make a mockery of you. I only desire to keep you from making a fool of yourself."

"Then I shall learn to dance." *Tell yourself that's all it is, sweet.* "In turn, you will learn from me the ways of lupine courtship."

"Courtship?" She laughed. "As I said, I am aware of what *courtship* entails. I take off my breeches and you shove your manhood into my maidenhead until you shudder to a close."

"It sounds rather unseemly when you put it that way."

She pointed at the part of him that remained hidden beneath her. "I looked at it while you slept. It hardly seemed the thing of poems and ballads. Besides, I am *not* mating you. Do not think you will trick me into your bed by disguising such acts as mere education."

"You misunderstand, Gerwalta. You wish to teach me a form for court dancing. I wish to show you a form of dancing to court."

"Then it is different for lupines."

He jerked his head up. "What is?"

"Nothing, no matter." Gerwalta rose, smoothing out the skirting of her tunic. "Do not joke, Andreas. Court dances are another form of diplomacy. They are not a child's game."

The werewolf licked his lips. "Neither is seduction."

Further discussion ceased as they both detected footfalls in the nearby brush. A string of expletives fled Francisco's tongue as he emerged from a patch of trees. He got one look at Andreas and threw his hands over his eyes.

"Pardon the gander, sir. I didn't expect to come back and find you... *occupied*."

Gerwalta and Andreas exchanged a look before the latter said, "No need for embarrassment, Francisco. Nudity is a common among lupines. But I can see it makes you uncomfortable. I'll dress."

"I thought I told you to wait until I returned?" Gerwalta accosted the layman as Andreas began to hunt for his clothing. "So, you left us behind on purpose? Why?"

"Begging your pardon, Fraulein, but it was the Spatar's command. He said I should check to make sure you hadn't torn each other up in the process of doing..."The stout man's cheeks blushed. "... whatever it was you two were about. Also, the Spatar thought, if there was danger, it may wish to trek out early today, unless, and I quote, 'they need more time to work out their differences.'"

Gerwalta's hands balled into fists. As Andreas pulled out his clothing from where he stored it in the undercarriage of the coach, he watched a narrative play out in the wolfsretter's expression. Frustration, confusion, realization and finally, determination.

He strolled over to her, put his hands on her shoulder. "I'm not going to ask what you're thinking, love. I just want to know that it doesn't end with my death or at the very least, castration."

"You are quite arrogant to suppose all my thoughts are of you," she spat back, pulling herself from his touch.

"Good, so I am safe." He turned to collect his shirt.

Gerwalta cackled. "Hardly."

SEVEN

Suggestions to make camp for the day went unheeded, and soon Gerwalta deduced why. It was a break in routine, giving her a chance to engage Karahan.

"I would ask to ride with the Spatar for a space, if you have no objection."

Andreas trudged along beside her, his eyes constantly scanning the forest. "What cause could I possibly have to object? Go, consign yourself to a confined space with a blood-thirsty dark one."

"Vampires are not known to feast on lupines or wolfsretters."

"My fields in Triberg are not often burdened by elephants either, but I wouldn't trust one to be released there."

She cackled. "Are you saying it is merely lack of opportunity, and that I may not go?"

"I do not nor would I ever tell you what you may or may not do. You're not my pack."

She couldn't resist an opportunity to tease. "And if I were your mate?"

He laughed into his shoulder. "I know what you *assume*. You think lupine husbands—*any* husband not a wolfsretter, is a domineering brute."

"You're saying you wouldn't be?"

"I told you before my mate shall be my equal. I would no more command you than you me, though I will strive always to stay in your good graces." He jerked his head to the coach rocking along the road behind him. "Go. If I hear anything concerning, I will not hesitate to rip his throat out."

A nod, and then Gerwalta turned and flagged Francisco to slow the horses. The door swung open after the first knock.

"Fraulein?"

Gerwalta pulled herself up on the riser. "May I pass some time with you, Spatar?"

The vampire looked up from a book spread on his lap, giving her a gracious smile. "You may, of course."

As soon as the door was closed, she eased into her inquisition. "I spotted a clocktower to the south. We are approaching another town."

The vampire resumed his study. "What of it?"

"Will you hunt there?"

The book stayed stationed, though his eyes rose to meet hers. "Why do you ask?"

She feigned loose interest. "A wolfsretter does not have much opportunity to learn of vampires and their habits, and I am cursed with curiosity. So far in our journey, when we've been in the proximity of a clocktower, you've gone off alone and come back looking much flusher. What is this city we are approaching, and why is it our destination? It cannot be Venice; it is not an island."

Though, given the time they'd been on the road, they *must* be getting closer.

"Venice is actually several islands." The book lowered. "This is Padua. We will stay with Messer Mazzi until it is time to advance into Venice."

"Padua? I have not heard of it." Her finger traced the bench beside her. "Still, it is good to have such friends. Do you have many, in many cities?"

Karahan's eyes narrowed. "Are you asking specifically, Fraulein Faust, about my friends in Nuremburg?"

She sat back, as though the distance would protect her. "I see the rumors are true; vampires can read thoughts."

The corners of his mouth rose along with a twinkle in his eye, and it amazed Gerwalta how this man—this dark one—could be so charmingly young and old at the same time.

"There is no reason for me to mislead you on this. Vampires

cannot read thoughts, though that is a common misconception. We can *plant* them, even ask one to reveal what he knows. Some minds are stronger than others, and some do not bend at all. Dark ones, for example, are immune from our skills."

"If you could not read my thoughts, then how did you know I intended to ask you of Nuremberg?"

"Your kind are not known as wanderers. When your mother mentioned you'd successfully completed a mission in Nuremberg, the imperial city, I suspected there may be unusual circumstances involved."

Gerwalta pondered a moment, playing out the consequences of withholding, or pursuing an adversarial tit-for-tat. Something about his revelation brought her to confess her own.

"There would be no reason for a vampire to journey to Ravensburg," she said. "It is a small town, barely more than a village, with no strategic importance to dark ones or the laymen. Something brought you there, and then to Triberg."

"Indeed." Karahan grinned and leaned in toward her. "Your theory?"

"While you were in Nuremberg, you spoke with the Emperor."

"I never said I was in Nuremberg."

"You did," she insisted. "You did not say 'if I have a friend in Nuremberg.' You said, 'are you asking about my friend in Nuremberg.' The statement tells me there are such friends to inquire about and citing it when I gave no pretense means it was the first place to come to *your* mind."

"What an intriguing intellect." The vampire's head seesawed as he pursed his lips. "Yes, I saw the Emperor, but I spoke not so much *with* him as *to* him."

"To what end?"

"Let's just agree that neither of us benefitted from his knowledge of our world. Now, he hasn't any."

A great knot in her stomach unwound for only a moment until she remembered what had driven her to speak with Karahan to begin with. "But you, I deduce, learned something from him about *me*."

His eyebrows arched. "Did I?"

She nodded. "You told Francisco to give Andreas and I some time alone to work out our differences."

"Is that what the youth call it these days? Differences?"

And there it was. "Despite what you may think, Spatar Karahan, there is nothing going on between Herr Baron and myself."

"He was awfully quick to volunteer himself for this mission when he learned you were the wolfsretter needing protection."

"I *do not* need protection." Nevermind that without Andreas's help, the surprise wolf attack may have worked. "I'll admit that the man is smitten with me, but that does not mean I reciprocate his feelings."

"You're either lying to me, Fraulein, or you're lying to yourself. Both, I'd venture." The vampire's eyes narrowed. "I have daughters too. I know the tricks a maiden plays to encourage her lover's attentions."

"Be that as it may, it does not mean I am such a maiden."

Any humor passed away from the vampire's face. "Your pulse ticks up every time he looks at you. Not only that, but it also ticks up when *you* look at *him*, even if he is unaware. There is also an inordinate amount of consideration and respect between you for two species so frequently opposed. I only joined fact with fancy."

His eyes turned to the window. "Also, a wolf I happened upon in Ravensburg told me a very curious story, of a hooded dark one who had saved him and others, lured away by an anathema wolf-queen, and who had amazingly admitted her love for a one of his kind in Nuremberg."

"I never admitted my love. I—"

Her words died on the air, even as her heart raced to explode. What had she done? *What had she done?*

"I mean that—What I *meant* to say is—"

The Spatar held up a hand. "I am not your Matron, Fraulein. You owe me no explanation, for I make no judgements on the aspirations of the heart."

"*You* may not, but every lupine and wolfsretter of good standing would." Fear emboldened her. Gerwalta reached out, setting her gloved hand on the vampire's knee. "Please, Spatar Karahan, I beg of you, tell no one what I've said, nor what you've seen. Within months I will be wed, and this situation will be consigned to the regrets of youthful indiscretion. But if it ever becomes known that anything happened between Andreas—*Herr Baron*—and I, he will be executed."

"That would be a terrifically poor use of a perfectly good alpha."

She blinked and retreated to her side of the cabin. "What did you call him?"

"An alpha. It is the common term for a konigswolf in the region from which I come. A bit gentler on the palate, I think." He rolled his tongue around in his mouth. "For all its linguistic tenacity, German is quite a severe language at the end of the day."

"I'm afraid I don't understand."

"I have no reason to disclose anything about your relationship to anyone," he continued undeterred. "You have my word, and I extend Francisco's by proxy of my powers. Neither of us will reveal your feelings for the wolf. But I must wonder, Fraulein, what are his intentions if he knows such a romance has deadly consequences?"

"The moment I understand the thoughts of the lovestruck, then I shall be the wisest woman who ever lived."

The vampire laughed. "Just a thought, Fraulein. If it truly is your intention to wed another and be a 'proper wolfretter' when you return, why not use this time away from judging eyes and loose tongues to indulge in that 'youthful indiscretion' rather than pull away from it? If you were immortal like me, I'd understand forbearance. But you are not; you will age and die. You have so very little time, when things come down to it. Do not waste it, and do not squander it for the sake of what anyone else thinks is proper. You will lie alone in your grave when you die regardless of with whom you share your bed whilst you live."

EIGHT

World weary, they entered town just after sunrise, as soon as the gates were thrown open. Whatever Nuremberg had been, Padua was just the same, minus an imperial palace. Covered in stone, crowded by smells and the people and animals responsible for them, even at an early hour, both lupine and wolfsretter felt it close in on them. At least it was not market day. That would have brought in a greater menagerie and clogged the passages of town.

Francisco pulled the coach to a stop and climbed down from his bench. "Are you at all ill, Herr Baron? You've gone quite white in the face."

Gerwalta stepped out of the coach at the same time, the first Andreas had seen of her in an hour. She'd dispelled her mystical red cloak, perhaps because the air here was not quite so cool as before, or perhaps because Karahan, familiar with the region and its customs, thought it ill-suited.

"Andreas?"

She rushed to his side at Francisco's words, hooking her arm through his and bringing him up to a proper stand. His beloved's attentions delivered magic, a primal refocus that reminded him they were far from home in a place surrounded by strangers. Instinct, roused by her touch, brought his attention to her well-being and moreover, her defense. Immediately, he straightened, scanning their surroundings, looking for a threat.

Francisco laughed. "Heavens be praised, Fraulein, you have a saint's touch. Look at how you called him back to himself." The coachman lifted a hand, adding from behind a smile, "Maybe you can cure me of my soreness from the ride?"

Rationality divorced itself from Andreas's actions, and he growled at the poor layman, whose arms immediately dropped to his side.

"Then again, maybe not."

Within a moment, Andreas recalled himself. Holy Mother, if a well-intentioned layman triggered this sort of defensiveness in him now, what was it going to be like once they were mated? Then again, she *was* drawing attention. Every man within sight of them pointed, speaking behind hands with each other.

"Herr Baron!" Gerwalta's light touch became a stinging grasp, her grip so tight around his forearm she threatened to break bone. "Do control yourself. Saints preserve, it isn't even near full moon! What the devil has gotten into you? It is only Francisco."

"I must concur with the lady, Herr Baron." Karahan stepped out of the coach and down into the street, despite the bright morn. "He is quite good at his job, and loyal to a fault. You can be assured, he has no intentions with her, despite what those lupine instincts suggest."

"Spatar Karahan?" Gerwalta looked to the coach, then to the vampire, repeated the process. "How are you not—"

"Bursting into flames?" Karahan completed for her. "I'm afraid, despite the stories, my kind doesn't do much bursting. We char after a while, eventually becoming stone, but the process takes time. The older the vampire, the shorter. Luckily, I'm only about three hundred."

Andreas demurred, looking to the footman who'd begun unloading boxes from atop the coach. "Apologies, Herr Francisco, the road was long and weariness dulls my civility."

Luckily the layman proved good-natured. "I dare say it does that to all God's creatures."

Karahan waved them up the street. "This way, now, children. I can be out in the sun a spell, but I do not enjoy it. Best to get off the streets before I crisp. It does tend to draw attention. Francisco, wait here with the horses and my goods. I will tell Messer Mazzi to send along his staff promptly to collect it and you."

"Yes, sir."

Moving swiftly towards one of the nearby residences, a stately rowhome built of stone and four stories tall, Karahan barked a laugh. "Come along now, Fraulein. I daresay Angelo will have a whole wardrobe of things you can wear that are less… let's say, suggestive."

Gerwalta examined herself. "My attire is overly modest if nothing else. What am I meant to believe it suggests?"

"It is well-suited to your nature and your calling, but I'm afraid in Padua, women to do not wear breeches in public. Only men do."

"So, they believe I'm a…" She stumbled with the words. "A crossdresser?"

"Yes, madame. Or worse, an actress."

Her hand landed on her chest. "I'm not sure which is worse. Very well, if I must wear a dress, then I shall. Only, I do not like how they are so open about the bottom."

As she pressed past, Andreas watched her backside, the rounded shape shifting with her legs, he hoped that whatever this Angelo Mazzi had, included many layers of undergarments and a generous number of peticoats, or he'd be thinking about that *opening* far too much.

As konigswolf, Andreas had never needed great wealth of knowledge of vampires or slayers. Still, he found himself questioning what little he did know. Seeing a vampire lord greet a slayer in the way of old friends, he wondered how foes managed to demonstrate such warmth. Wherein, aside from Gerwalta, every wolfsretter he'd ever known had considered him a pest worthy of loathing.

Wolfsretters and lupines could learn from their city cousins.

After embracing their host with genuine amenity, Karahan extended an arm and swept the air back to where he and Gerwalta stood in wait, moving his tongue away from Italian.

"Messer Angelo Mazzi of the Solari Padua, may I present my companions on this quest: King Andreas Baron of the Triberg Pack, and the Righteous Fraulein Gerwalta Faust, Fourth Daughter of Gunda Faust, Matron of the House of Red."

Andreas had expected to find a man with light skin and a round countenance for some reason. That's how he thought of the sun, and shouldn't a creature which harnessed its power be of like appearance? A silly thought, he realized, taking in the high cheek bones, silky ebony locks, and olive skin of a man even his packling shewolves would go crimson over.

Mazzi's blue eyes grew wide as he hastened to bend at the waist. "Your highnesses, welcome. It is a great honor to host you."

Gerwalta let out a little grasp. "You speak German."

"I do, Fraulein. I speak many languages," he concurred, righting himself. "Slayers often study many tongues, as vampires tend to move about. You'll find very few vampires in the Doge's palace are native to this region. Most travel the Mediterranean's great cities. Athens, Istanbul, Cairo…"

"The Doge of Venice entertains vampires?"

The slayer shook his head. "Oh, not *that* Doge. No, the layman Doge, Nicolo Sagredo may host the occasional pirate or Medici, but he minds the laity and is, as far as I know, unaware of the ebb and flow of the undead in his city. Luciana Martelli, the vampire doge, on the other hand…."

Andreas's mouth dropped. "The vampire doge is a… woman?"

He didn't have to look at Gerwalta to feel the burn of her glare, as though questioning a female in a position of power was an insult meant for her. He couldn't help it though; lupines were patriarchal, and the last exception he'd seen to that had nearly cost him his life.

"Oh, yes, and quite a woman at that." A blush rose in the slayer's cheeks, one that spread to Gerwalta's as she met his eyes.

Do not growl. Do not growl.

"But that is neither here nor there. You must be quite tired after being on the road so long. Knowing my old friend, I'm willing to bet Igor kept pushing you on, not letting you stop in a real place with a real bed for…. How long did the journey take from the Schwarzwald, a fortnight?"

"Igor?" Andreas turned on the vampire. "I thought your name was Goran Karahan?"

It was the slayer who answered in the bluster of an explosive hack. "Is *that* what he's calling himself? Saints preserve us, Igor, where did you come up with that one?"

Karahan blanched, demurring his head. "I do wish you'd respect my privacy, my friend. A persona is no easy thing to cultivate, and I would not have mine thrown out with the ease of turned milk."

"Ah, bash with that!" The Italian stepped forward, draping an arm over Gerwalta and Andreas, taking them underwing. "Welcome to my home, my new friends. Rest, relax, and this evening at dinner, I will tell you all the dark little secrets Igor wishes would wash away with time. Then, I will pull out my finest spirits, and we will taunt sobriety until morning. Yes, it will be a grand evening indeed."

NINE

There was a great deal of difference between wearing a *dress*, which Gerwalta did with little complaint, and wearing whatever contrived device this was, the application of which required assistance from two of Mazzi's female servants and a saint's patience. Wool stockings, drawers, petticoats, a corset, stays, an odd kind of bustle that came in a pair and were worn off the hips instead of the rear… and that was just all the things that went underneath the preposterous silk coverlet on the outside!

"Do female slayers wear such things?" Gerwalta asked the girl who spoke French.

Bernice translated the question to her fellow lady's maid, which prompted the other to say something back that set both giggling.

"What are you laughing about?"

The smile on the servant's face fizzled. "Apologies, mademoiselle, but it's only… Well, Portia said that they do, but they don't wear it for very long."

Suddenly, her garments felt tighter and looser at the same time.

The fire on the hearth flickered as the air in the room shifted. Both servants leapt to their feet as the door opened and a huffing Andreas plowed into the room.

"This is a bone too far!"

The servants fled, making for the door as Andreas planted himself before Gerwalta, holding his arms akimbo. "Look at me. *Look at me!* A wig? I am expected to wear *a wig*. And that's just the start of what is wrong. Have you ever heard of a lupine donning silk stockings? And what kind of breeches only come down to the knee? Don't even get me started about this coat! It looks like I'm wearing a skirt, like I'm some sort of shewolf in heat. And…"

"Andreas!"

It was at that precise moment that his eyes finally fell upon her, and with that, his tongue stilled.

"Look at *me*." She attempted to walk forward and found the task impossible without a great deal of swooshing. "Do you think I am without complaint? I don't know if I'm going to dinner or blowing out to sea."

His eyes traced the outlines of her bodice which, unlike the lower half of her body buried in a veritable mound of pink silk, fitted tight, enhancing the feminine flip of her hips.

And, because the dress was Italian, pressed her breasts into a cruel form of submission, both constricting and framing them.

The beast in him salivated.

Gerwalta snapped her fingers, breaking the lupine's concentration to her womanly assets. "Herr Baron!"

He sparked to attention, regaining her eyes. "Sorry, did you say something?"

Wolves were such men.

Or was it the other way around?

"I quite understand your issue, but no doubt we are not to be subjected to Italian clothing as a mere means of torture. Remember, vampires are city creatures, and they like to put on airs. It will be much easier to corner our prey if we blend in with its environment. I daresay if I wore my red cloak, and you your farmer's frock, these vampires we are to trap would see us coming from some distance away. Consider this practice."

The lust dissolved in the wake of the practical. "But how are we to move in this attire? If I were to take my fur whilst dressed up in this ninny-wear, I'm as likely to find myself trapped as not. Silk is not unlike a wolfsretter: soft to the touch, thin to the eye, but tough as iron when tested by force."

"That almost sounded like a compliment. Was it intentional?"

He grimaced. "I have never disrespected your kind's capacity or strengths. It is a fool of a konigswolf who would do so."

Every time she wanted to be surprised by what he'd said, she found herself more astounded still by *why* he'd said it.

"Be that as it may, I believe we are obligated for the moment to, as the saying goes, do as the Romans do. Let's make the best of it we can."

Her arms went out, falling gently on the air, as she prepared her opening pose.

The werewolf huffed. "Now? You wish to teach me dances *now*? You add insult to injury, Walta."

"Our sojourn is nearly half-over already. How many more opportunities will we have? Mazzi's maids said dinner isn't for another hour; it is a sufficient time to practice."

He crossed his arms over his chest. "I take no issue with playing a court jester before the wolfsretter. It is no insult to my person to be thought of as ignorant of courtly ways. I am."

"But you agreed to this! I will not have you made to look the fool, even if you would not feel it."

"Why would *you* care how they perceive me?"

Implication weighed heavy in his word. Fine, if that's what it took to bring the wolf into submission, she'd give a little in his direction.

"Just because I refuse to indulge your unrealistic fantasy of our union does not mean I do not care for you at all. You may be willing to endure the slings and arrows of my family's insults, but it won't be on my watch."

She assumed a position before the fireplace. "First, the bow. Left foot forward, then back, then bend slightly at the knees."

The demonstration came in time with the instruction, and though he allowed one more look of concern, he soon gave in. To her delight, he proved an apt pupil, quick to learn and ready to please. In short order, Andreas had become the master of La Volta and passed reasonably well on the Allemande, though all her instruction suffered from the fact that they were just one couple and without music. Though Gerwalta attempted to explain different rotations, she knew from experience nothing replaced reenactment.

"And we end, as we began, with a bow." She demonstrated proper form, but when she raised her eyes, she found Andreas standing straight, gawking.

She looked down at her attire, wondering if in all their swishing and swaying, one of her stays had come undone.

"What is it?"

Andreas reached out, taking her hand. "If I wasn't a lupine, I'd never know you were not a laywoman. You can look and act just like one of them. How did you learn all this anyhow?"

"My family's trade takes us into laymen circles from time to time. Though occasions have been few for me, I was still given the proper education if need ever arose for me to entertain guests."

"Wearing something like—" Andreas motioned broadly at her. "—this tent?"

She laughed. "No, we don't fancy ourselves capable of Venetian fashion in the Schwarzwald."

"Thank the Lord Almighty. How do these Italians manage to reproduce in such quantities with such troublesome clothing?"

"Andreas!" She tried to hide her smile behind her hands, but her laugh eked out all the same.

The wolf had no shame. "Do not tell me the thought did not occur to you."

"It most certainly did not."

"Liar!" He pulled her hands away, drinking in the humor of her eyes. When they met, the laughter dissolved, and looking anywhere else would have taken herculean effort.

He stepped closer, dropping her hands and placing his on the crown of the bustles hiding her hips. "It was the first thing I thought when I walked in and saw you in this. I said to myself, 'Andreas, you want to ravish this creature, that much is plain, but how would you go about it?'"

"With a great deal of effort, I would suppose."

He stepped closer. "Do you suppose they would bounce if you

wore them while making love?"

"I do."

His hands slid up her sides, the silk tickling her under his fingers. "We should endeavor to learn."

She withdrew moments before his lips reached hers, parading across the room in a huff.

"*Enough!* Why must you constantly tempt my resolve? I am a strong woman, but I am not unbreakable. Please stop encouraging my affections."

"Perhaps, love, you are unaware that the point of seduction *is* to encourage affections."

"But seduction to what end?" She threw up her arms. "Why are you so determined to sacrifice yourself to win me, when you'd lose me and your life *by* winning?"

"Dearest Walta, do you not realize that your love is worth dying for?" He stepped forward, taking her right hand between his own and raising it to his mouth. Andreas's lips caressed the bare knuckles. "You left me alone for a year in hopes that my love for you would fade. It has not. It *cannot.* I am here on this earth to love you. If that means my death, I am already dead. You are not saving me by denying me; you're subjecting me to purgatory."

"There is no future in which we can be together."

"Love, we are together *now.*"

It ended there: her ill wishes, her spite, her arguments, her resistance. The wolfsretter crashed into him, pressing her lips to his, her arms thrown around his neck. The force of her person and her wardrobe were more than the lupine was expecting, but he saved himself from toppling over in time to catch her legs as she jumped up to encircle him at the hip.

And then, without warning, she was gone.

His eyes flew open, prepared to see Gerwalta performing the type of emotional acrobatics that was becoming her calling card, but what he discovered was much worse:

His love was pressed against the wall, her arms high overhead and held by a pair of ghostly white hands.

And a vampire was feeding at her throat.

TEN

Andreas let loose the beast, the pain wracking his every limb, anguish tormenting his bones and breaking his body into pieces until another creature took its place. The feat was achieved in the flap of a gnat's wing. Andreas leapt forward, instinctively set to devour that which threatened what was his.

Kill him.

All wolves knew the legend: that there had once been a time before slayers and wolfsretter, when vampires and werewolves stood on opposite sides of the battle, enemies to the last. He felt that truth now beat as his own heart, driving him to murder, to rend, to destroy.

But wolves were meant to fight in packs, not solitarily and inside a lady's chamber.

The vampire's head flew back as Andreas's maw wrapped around his leg, rending muscle and hitting bone. It was the oddest duality: the taste of something dead, the sweetness of fresh meat. It danced in glory upon his tongue as none other had. The evisceration ended abruptly as the vampire moved with speed lightning would envy. The creature streaked across the room, pulling along the complicated set of dresses, bustles, and underthings that entombed Gerwalta Faust.

He still tasted her, followed the scent as it streaked through the house, the growl rumbling in his chest. Despite the power and agility of this body, wolves were not meant to be graceful in doors. A side table in a hall toppled over as he rounded a corner, shattering whatever dish or vase had rested upon it. Andreas hit the stairs just in time to see Gerwalta's feet disappear.

"What is going on?"

"Vampire, and a hostile one."

The konigswolf did not slow when he heard voices behind him. Mazzi and Karahan bit his heels as he reached the top step, both the vampire and the slayer quicker on two feet somehow then he managed on four.

"Which way, Herr Baron?"

The Spatar looked to him for direction, and Andreas was happy to provide.

A hall, a chamber, a balcony.

A jump. The roof of the neighboring home.

Red tiles cracked and slipped under his feet as Andreas tried to shore up his footing. No use; as his limbs explored every cardinal direction, they displaced more tiles in each one. Finally, the only direction his legs could go was down. Andreas barked, then yelped as his body filled the hole. He had not fallen through, but he also had nothing beneath him against which to gain leverage and rise out. He wondered if the occupant of the home in whose roof he was now pegged could see his paws dangling from their ceiling, and what they may think of that.

Mazzi rounded him with ease, holding up a hand. *Much good that will do,* Andreas thought. *Slapping cannot be a very successful defense against vampires.*

Only, the Italian *didn't* slap Gerwalta's captor. He didn't even touch him. What he did do was so much more amazing.

Mazzi *made* sunlight appear in the dark of night.

The vampire's grip went slack as he threw his hands over his face, releasing Gerwalta in the process. The wolfsretter, despite her excessive wardrobe, gained a solid stance. As she moved, however, Andreas understood she hovered more than stood. Not a single tile slipped beneath her, and the ridiculous dress had enough slack to help her pull off the deception. The vampire, however, could not hover and had been rendered blind. Consquently, he fell to all fours to keep from toppling backward off the roof. The act told Andreas two things: one, he was not the only dark one challenged by heights. And two, this vampire still feared falling. He was fresh from his creche and unfamiliar with the resilience of his immortal body.

Mazzi's steps fell like dew. "You're not from the Vicenze creche. Who sent you and why are you here?"

The vampire only shook his head.

The ball of light dancing on the Italian's hand increased the slightest increment. "I take it you've never met one of my kind, then. You do know at this range, I need merely to flick this your direction and you will die, do you not? But I can see you are new to your fangs. I have some sympathy for your ignorance. Tell me what I want to know, and I'll let you live."

Was he insane? Gerwalta wasn't some innocent girl snatched from the shadowy street; she was attacked inside the home of a slayer. What possible goal could the vampire have but to kill her, and quite on purpose? Did Helga's influence extend all the way here? If so, how would she know where to find them?

The vampire buried his head between his hands. "I was sent to kill her. She is my first blood."

The slayer looked back over his shoulder at Karahan, who kept a safe distance, lingering in the window of Mazzi's home.

"My friend, any chance he is born of your line?"

Karahan shook his head. "But that does not mean he has not fallen under the Ravens' influence."

"Then you'd have no objection to my killing him?"

"I wouldn't even if he were a Dracule." A sinister hue Andreas had not noticed before gleamed in the Spatar's eyes. "I disavowed any of my son's progeny, just as I disavowed him."

Without removing his proxy hold of the assailant, Mazzi chuckled. "If only that let you kill the whelp yourself."

Gerwalta had grown tired of prattle. In a blink, she summoned silver—in which of her many bolts of fabric had that been hiding, he'd like to know—and had created a blade. She crossed the vampire, anchored her hands on his scalp, and pulled him to his feet. His back leaned into her shoulder.

"Who sent you?" she demanded, pushing her blade to the base of his throat. "Who wants me dead?"

"You're wasting your time," Karahan called from the window. "He's a sapling of a vamp executing the order of his creche, not so unlike your wolves obeying the orders of a king. This vampire is too new to the fang to have a mind of his own. He's obviously been ordered to stay silent, and silent he will stay.”

Andreas would not believe it himself if he didn't see it, but Gerwalta growled her frustration. No sooner had it registered—the sound stirring a desire that was bordering more by the day on need—than she pressed the dagger into the vampire's flesh, drawing a slow, molasses-like drop of undead blood.

“Fine, then. Tell me who gave you the order.”

“I'd do it, son,” Mazzi patronized. “Fraulein Faust here is a daughter of the infamous House of Red. You'll be no less dead if she cuts off your head then if I hit you with my solarium.”

“I'll die anyway if I come back without her life beating in my veins.”

What did that mean, “her life beating in my veins”? Surely nothing pleasant. Not for the first time, Andreas worked his legs, hoping to at least rock himself backward enough to free a limb. If he could just get one paw on the roof proper, pushing himself backward with the aid of the angles would assure his freedom. Just as he felt the tiniest leverage, something grabbed him at the paw.

Everything that followed happened instantaneously. Gerwalta let go her captive, diving in Andreas's direction. The vampire in turn pursued her. Mazzi's sun-ball flew, attempting to keep the latter from reaching the former. Something yanked at his leg, pulling him through the hole he'd created and filled.

A shudder of black cloth, and then, blackness itself as he fell into the dark of the void beneath his feet.

ELEVEN

As a dark one, sunlight and Gerwalta had never been kindreds. When she dove in the direction of Andreas's disappearing body and the ball of energy Messer Mazzi had conjured whizzed by her en route to the vampire, she too felt its burn. The crackle of the flame and the hum of the energy blistered her arm, despite missing her completely. It must be strong enough to kill the vampire who'd attacked her. Only, when she landed on the roof near the hole that had swallowed the konigswolf and turned back to make sure the enemy was vanquished, she found her expectations spoiled.

Where the vampire had been, a silver shield as tall as a grown man stood, the billow of a black cloak fanning out behind it.

"Impossible."

But it wasn't. In fact, given time to reason, she'd have found it quite logical. Why should the interloper not be here? Because he was a wolfsretter? That had not prevented *her*, had it? Venice—as far as she was aware, the entire peninsula—fell under the control of the purview of the Yellow bloodline. What was a wolfsretter from the House of Night doing in Italy? Their region was that of the Safavid and Ottoman empires, not the West.

Little time was afforded her to absorb the shock of another of her kind having deflected the blow. Fingers of gray smoke funneled through the air with much too much deliberation. In a few blinks, the mass condensed and took shape. Behind the opposing wolfsretter, her assailant, found himself braced by two vampires of unnatural muscular endowment. Each held his arms in a manner that made the attacker grimace.

Good, at least he'd gotten some unpleasantness.

"Messer Mazzi," the one on the left said, he of flaxen hair and a noble countenance.

"Messer Brunelli," the slayer returned, adding on further words in Italian that made no sense to her. But as Gerwalta relaxed her ear, she found certain ones stood out due to their similarities to French. Slowly, meaning began to take shape.

Disobeyed… Confusion… Apologies…

Andreas was a konigswolf; she knew the fall into the house did not harm him, and now that their enemy seemed neutralized, she meant to get to the bottom of what had happened.

"Are you attempting to say," she cut into Mazzi and Brunelli's conversation in her most formal German, unsure if she'd be understood by the vampire, "that what has happened here was some kind of misunderstanding?"

The handsome man's violet eyes shifted her way. "*Non parla la nostra lingua?*"

"I do not believe she does," Mazzi answered in German. "Fraulein Faust comes from the Schwarzwald."

His German dripped with Italian seasonings, but all the same… "*Scuzi,* Fraulein, but as I was telling Messer Mazzi, this young one misunderstood his directions. On behalf of our master, I offer you my humblest apologies for the inconvenience."

"Having fangs sunk into my neck is not what I would call an *inconvenience.*" She straightened. "Who is your master? I am owed restitution for this *misunderstanding.*"

Mazzi skirted to Gerwalta's side, speaking into her shoulder. "Fraulein, please. Brunelli is the Doge's second in command, as well as her consort of two decades. His apology is her apology." He cleared his throat before continuing in amplified tones so that all may hear. "We accept in anticipation."

Brunelli bowed. "We are delighted this could be resolved without further conflict." He didn't look delighted, particularly as he scowled in Gerwalta's direction. "We hope that we can still expect you tomorrow evening for *la Carnivale?*"

"Messer Brunelli, it is the highlight of my year."

The Doge's second turned back to her. "I will send a new dress, Fraulein, to replace the one this fool so shamelessly stained with blood. I look forward to dancing with you tomorrow night."

"To dancing with…." Her voice sputtered as formality loosened itself from her grip. Gerwalta was not unskilled in the art of diplomacy, but she was not its most ardent fan. The wolfsretter plastered a dulcet smile upon her face and recalled the silver in her grip from its service. The metal licked back up her arms and plated itself in ringlets around her forearm. "Messer Brunelli…"

"Please, call me Massimo."

Gerwalta tried not to gag. If this rogue thought he could deter her with flattery… "Very well, then. *Massimo,* I have been a member of my own court long enough to know misunderstandings do, on occasion, occur. But mark my words, there can be no confusion. This vampire attacked me and clearly told us he had been sent to dispatch of me. What part of that was the result of misinterpretation?"

Massimo did not waver for a moment, letting a cocky grin cover his face. "I intend to find out come sunrise. I suspect, however, that he errantly believed he was meant to subdue and capture *you.*"

But if not her, then who? The respect, if only ceremonial, that Massimo showed for Messer Mazzi suggested they were on agreeable turns.

Like a clock striking twelve, everything sank into place, and just who the assailant had been dispatched to collect became all too clear.

Andreas! She ran for the last place he'd been…and stopped. A queer sensation tickled her insides, and its identification drove her to double her speed when she resumed.

A sliver of moonlight from the half-disk in the sky peeked down, sending a searchlight into the darkness below. Gerwalta's eyes lingered beyond the hole through which the wolf had fallen only long enough to let her adjust and her heart shatter.

He was not there. The werewolf who not two minutes ago had plummeted from view, had disappeared completely.

She regained her feet and spun on her heel, even as the unwelcome undead dissolved into clouds of smoke and the wolfsretter jumped from the roof, disappearing against the dark of night.

"What have you done with him!" Gerwalta's feet cracked slate with each step she bolted, chasing the pillars as they snaked through the air.

"Fraulein, stop! You'll fall."

The slayer's arms caged her from behind just as her foot reached the edge of the roof.

"I will not. I will…"

"Fall to your death is what you'll do," Messer Mazzi said as he yanked her back. "Unless you can fly."

But she *could* fly….

But who knew who could be watching? The wolfsretter from the House of Night may still be lingering within view. True to their legend, he may be hidden in plain sight, invisible to any but those by whom he wished to be seen. And if anyone found out, her hopes for getting away from Triberg would be gone. She'd do anything to protect her secret, even let Andreas be taken.

And that proved why she didn't deserve him.

But she'd be damned if she wasn't going after him, because *he* didn't deserve *that*.

Gerwalta ceased her flailing and allowed herself to be pulled back. "This is the second time Andreas has allowed himself to be captured away from me, and by god, it's going to be the last."

"Whatever they want him for, Fraulein, it is not death. At least, not immediately, or else that black hood would have run him through with his silver instead of shielding the sapling."

She couldn't disagree, but if they weren't after killing Andreas, what did they want him for?

TWELVE

"Drink this. It will help with the nerves."

Red liquid swirled inside of a green-tinted glass pressed to her palm.

"I am not nervous, Messer Mazzi." Gerwalta looked up from the offering. "I am furious."

The blond-haired Italian sputtered. "Surely, Fraulein, you do not think *I* had anything to do with this."

"No, I do not." She turned to Karahan sitting by the fireplace, his eyes chasing flames. "But I believe *you* did."

Even the reasoning had seemed off to her at the beginning. Why would *she* need a bodyguard? Gerwalta had dismissed Karahan's patronizing; all men thought women weak. Except the wolfsretter, where females bested their male counterparts in strength and cunning. So why have a wolf along to protect her?

Because that wasn't why he was there.

Gerwalta stood and paced toward the fire. "Was it true, what you told my mother? What you told me?"

"Everything was true." He sipped at his own wine before adding under his breath, "I simply did not tell you the *whole* truth."

She set the unsampled drink down on a nearby table and settled into a comfortable position. "I will have it, then."

"Have what?"

"The *whole* truth, Spatar." She leaned forward. "Now."

Karahan passed her an amused smirk. "How old are you, Fraulein?"

"I hardly see what *that* has to do with any—"

In a flash, he was upon her, his fangs bared, the gruesome creature he kept hidden within unleashed and a breath from her throat.

"Watch yourself, Igor," the slayer said from behind. "We are old friends, but I'll not hesitate to kill you if you attack this young woman."

"It is exactly because she is young that I do this." His tongue flicked out, licked the hollow of her throat. "You taste as if you've barely come into your womanhood. Now, how old are——"

"Twenty-two!" The words came of their own volition, the fear palpable on her lips. "I was twenty-two last December. I am no child."

"You are to me!" the vampire spat, before spinning on his heel and going to stand again by the fire. "I have walked this earth for over three hundred years. I have lauded saints and I have fostered sinners. I have overthrown the men of God, and I have fought under the banner of gods of men. I *know* what evil is, Fraulein. I birthed it that cursed night in Istanbul when, young in my fangs, I birthed *him*."

"Birthed him?" she gasped. "Birthed who?"

Karahan spit his name out like a curse. "Vlad Tepes."

She knew the name. Curse her, but she knew the name. "The Prince of Blood? But he's dead!"

"Do you think I'd risk your life and mine if he was?" A gristly laugh rattled in the vampire's chest. "No, Vlad is very much alive."

She grabbed the glass and downed the contents in one tremendous gulp. "But what does this have to do with Andreas?"

Here, Messer Mazzi picked up the thread. "All invitees are expected to pay tribute," he said. "The Doge demands that each vampire paterfamilias supply."

"And this year, she asked for wolves." Gerwalta put together the rest for herself. She turned to Mazzi. "Then you did know of this."

He turned away in shame. "I *suspected*. The friendship Igor and I have been able to share is only possible because we've learned when to be curious and when to mind our own business. It is a necessary balance, as our natures are so inherently opposed to each other."

She looked at Mazzi, at Karahan, back at Mazzi.... "Tell me this then: why come all the way to the Schwarzwald to collect a lupine? Why travel all the way to Triberg when you yourself admitted to encountering the pack in Ravensburg? It would have made for a shorter trip."

"Of course, I could have snatched one from anywhere. I came to the Schwarzwald not for Herr Baron," Karahan admitted, "I came for you."

Her innards lurched. "Why am I so special?"

"Because I am not a cruel man," he said. "I could have contracted any wolfsretter to bond my sons in silver, but how to save all the wolves brought in chains to the Doge's Palace?"

The wolfsretter's heart threatened to burst. "You mean the wolves are in danger?"

"I believe so, yes." An open gaze bespoke wonderment, respect, hope. It was such an odd look, one that she rarely saw on anyone's face, let alone a dark one's. "While chasing down one of Vlad's plots, I found myself in Nuremberg and heard the story of a young wolfsretter with blazing red hair and an explementary heart, who rescued wolves from a corrupted alpha female, and I knew… I knew!… that *that* woman would be the one who could deliver both the dark ones and the laity from my mistakes."

The weight of expectation settled heavy on her shoulders, collapsing her lungs. Gerwalta struggled to breathe. "I should have killed the laymen who witnessed my misdeeds."

"There is no need, Fraulein. I remade their memories. One did get away, but often the rants of a single man carry the weight of the air he exhales in making them." He crossed from the fire, lifted her chin. "But please know, what you did in Nuremberg was no misdeed. It was an act of compassion rarely seen in your kind, and I need you to have that level of conviction again."

She swallowed down her emotions, making mincemeat of his flattery. "You hired me to trap vampires, Spatar, not lose the man I love."

"Save him, then, and the others who've fallen victim to Vlad's plots."

"And in turn, will you save me?"

"Save you?" His hand pulled away, as though she'd suddenly lit on fire. "From what?"

She leaned to the side, locking the silent slayer in her gaze. "Messer Mazzi, would you say that the Doge's court is highly politicized?"

"Is it not the underpinnings of a royal court to be so?" he laughed.

Ah, Italians and their humor. "Did you take *Massimo's* explanation as Bible truth?"

"Ah, yes, I see what you're getting at." Mazzi stood. "I believe that the vampire who attacked you was acting on someone's order, though I trust Massimo did not know of it."

For the first time in their acquaintance, Karahan was thrown for a loop. "What does that mean? What is she getting at?"

"This is the second time that someone has attempted to kill me since we left Triberg," Gerwalta said. "My would-be assassin wants me dead, but only by a means in which their touch would not be felt."

Karahan shook his head. "It is merely coincidence."

"Coincidence is never coincidence." Her tattered dress wreaked of vampire. Torn to threads as parts were, beyond the repair of even the most talented of seamstresses, what shame was there in removing the outside layer and throwing it to the flames? "I don't believe your finding me was an act of your own doing, Herr Spatar, though I'm quite sure the plots were engineered for you to think so. Vampires were behind the plot to expose lupines to the Holy Roman Empire, but a vampire would have no need for confiscation in targeting me, nor would a wolf know the truth of my acts. No, it is one of my own who wants me dead, and as you're using me to solve your problems, they're using you to solve theirs."

"But what problem could another wolfsretter have with you?" Karahan asked. "And how would they learn all this anyhow?"

She had no idea on the first part, but the second made perfect sense. "Spatar Karahan, what led you to Nuremberg?"

He hesitated. There must be such a measure of light he'd bring to matters he'd prefer left in the dark. Only when her gaze burrowed into him did Karahan relent.

"I don't know how familiar you are with the House of Night,

Fraulein. Before Vlad decided to engineer the genocide of lupines himself, he first tried to get them to do it. They refused, and in retaliation, Vlad raided their silver mines in the Degirmencik province. I simply followed the path of that silver as it came north, and into the coffers of the Holy Roman Emperor."

"Through my cousin Bernhardt's effort," she said when he'd finished. "The Vicematron of Ravensburg was a woman named Maria Dreger, Bernhardt's mother. After my mission to Nuremberg, she was called in for questioning. My mother relinquished her of her position and vanquished her, but Maria was found dead the next day. Someone in the House of Red did it, though no one has owned it."

"And then you were attacked soon after we left the Schwarzwald. Karahan's mouth fell open. "Someone in your mother's court wants you dead, too. Do you know who?"

"I have suspicions, yes, but knowing she is behind the plot does not tell me who will execute it here."

Mazzi puckered his lips, then nodded. "Massimo Brunelli might know."

Gerwalta turned on the slayer. "Why?"

"Massimo wants you there in the open. His invitation in front of others meant as much. He had meant for you to be sneaked in."

"He meant for me to be concealed?" A student of conspiracy and intrigue, she did so hate that she hadn't anticipated this. "The Doge's second in command is one of your conspirators?"

Mazzi nodded. "Who better to cut off the head than the very hand which bears the weapon?"

A cannonball exploded in Gerwalta's ribs as she realized just how true a statement that was.

She continued, "Even if I carry out this act and trap the Ravens, I will arrive home a corpse if those communicating with Triberg are not exposed. Part of your plan involves the capture of Tepes and his men. The other, overseeing their imprisonment. I cannot assure that if I am dead."

Karahan, it seemed, was not the type to renegotiate terms. His temple wrinkled as he turned on her. "Then I suggest that you not die.

Your internal court politics is none of my concern. I have already agreed to a blood debt to your mother. If she wished it paid, that is for her to decide. For now, I expect you to save yourself."

And with that, he smoked from the room.

THIRTEEN

Andreas bit in the direction of whatever had him by the ankle, but that only made things worse. Silver thread looped around his maw, drawing it closed. A moment later, the binding roped his paws as well. The lupine was bound and tied like a pig being readied for market.

The animal within recognized its predictament, and Andreas gave into instinct. Thrashing, he tried to loosen his restraints; the act drove the bindings deeper, nesting into his fur, the silver blistering flesh upon contact.

"If you want your love to live, calm yourself!"

The words were German, but the speaker was not—nor, given the slant of the foreign tongue, was he Italian.

Andreas finally overrode his wolf hearing the words. He'd vie for his own freedom, even if that meant drawing blood, but he would not do so if it meant bringing any harm to Gerwalta. He stilled, turning to search the darkness for his captor. A form took shape against the darkness, more a silhouette than a person. Only when his eyes refused to focus further did he understand the truth of what he was seeing, though clarity did not partner with belief. After all, being from the Schwarzwald, the konigswolf had never seen a wolfsretter not born of the House or Red, let alone one of the House of Night.

The man removed his black hood, showing that the coloration did not end with his attire. His sable hair fell in gentle curls that kissed his shoulders. Inkwell eyes stared at him, peering out from a face clouded by a thick beard and patches of skin the color of parched earth.

A shiver went down the length of the wolf's ridge. He let his body go lax. There was no point in fighting.

"Good." The corner of the dark man's mouth rose. "I'm going to remove your restraints and you will come with me with haste and without sound. Do as I say, and I swear to you, the red hood will not be harmed."

Without the ability to fly unto the roof and protect Gerwalta himself, what could he do? As soon as he was free of the bonds, despite the sting left where silver had touched his skin, Andreas rose to all fours and followed.

Wolves were not intended to ride in coaches. That much became clear as they whisked through Padua and rode toward the sea.

"Are you certain you would not take your lay form?" the wolfsretter asked as he stepped into a boat that was thrice the length of its width. "I do have clothing here in the boat for you. If modesty is your concern...."

Andreas shifted into his skin without another thought, drawing wide eyes from the oarmen who began to recite the rosary.

The lupine pointed at the terrified laymen. "Your oarsman is not in the fold?"

"He is an employee of the Doge, but there are few lupines in Venice. It's likely the first time he's ever witnessed a transformation. That or...."The wolfsretter's eyes raked down the plains of Andreas's hard stomach, coming to rest on the rise of hips. "Are all wolves in your pack so liberal with your nudity? This is Venice, Herr Baron, not Florence." He grabbed a drape of clothing from behind him and threw it up to Andreas on the quay. "Cover yourself."

The distance between the island—or *islands* as he discovered when they neared—did not last much, but by the measure of its culture, it was like a new world. With rare exception, stone and masonry covered all land. Houses, churches, and cobblestone streets collapsed in on each other. The oarsman guided them first from the shore to open waters, then into a great channel which divided the sectors of town into three primary masses, and into a series of smaller and smaller canals.

Their boat slipped through in the night, lit only by the long torch affixed to a post rising from the prow, passing under an occasional bridge that joined pathways overhead. No matter how he attempted, Andreas's eye could catch little of these pedestrian lanes, for their byways in turn twisted, as though the city had been planned and laid down by the roots of a mighty tree and not the whims of men.

"Everything is packed together so tightly."

"Yes, it reminds one of Istanbul."

Andreas turned upon the wolfsretter to find a like look of growing apprehension. "Is that where you are from?"

"If only."

"If not there, then where?"

The dark man laughed. "It is… not for me to discuss."

"And what is?" Andreas said. "Where are you taking me, and to what end?"

"That is also not for me to discuss." The wolfsretter leaned over the side of the boat, dipping his gloved finger in the water. "My tongue knows a thousand tales, and in each of them, a dagger."

With one more bend behind them, the boat pulled alongside one of the buildings. Between two poles which stuck out of the water and served as breakers, a small dock extended. The man who assisted them unto land beared fangs as both passed; Andreas ignored him. He was here only long enough to discover what threat a wolfsretter of the House of Night represented and disarm any who may threaten Gerwalta. Tossing fur with a fanged parasite may be necessary, but he'd not engage in it unless forced.

"What is this place?"

The wolfsretters led the way through an opulent courtyard decorated by marble statues and roses. "The Doge's Palace. It does not matter; you are not here to see her."

A new voice spoke. "No, you are not."

Regal. Terrible. Powerful. Deadly.

The man who descended from the grand central staircase was dressed in black finery and wearing his family's coat of arms molded in gold on his chest. The vampire took each step with deliberate precision, as though prowling. His pale skin contrasted with the black hair which ran in streams over his shoulders. Andreas's inner wolf rumbled, fight or flight instincts difficult to subdue. The animal within recognized a predator—the man, an advisory.

The new arrival continued. "There are many faults with the ways of my kind, in my opinion, but some demented conception that only men are capable to rule is not one. Once in a blue moon, an odd female *can* be worthy. Nor do we, like the wolfsretter, automatically declare the so-called fairer sex superior. Every vampire lives and dies on the merits of his or her own abilities, be it strength, cunning, or an acumen to reign. Luciana Morelli, third vampire Doge of Venice, excels in all three."

"And you?" Andreas squared his shoulders, turned toward the vampire. "What do you excel in?"

"Dominating Luciana." He extended his arm, surprising Andreas with a gesture of neutrality. "Welcome to Venice. I am Vlad Tepes of the Dracule bloodline."

"Andreas Baron, Konigswolf of Triberg." Not knowing how else to respond, Andreas met the gesture in kind. "Why am I here, Herr Tepes?"

The vampire grinned, even as he turned and invited by a sweep of his hand for Andreas to follow, the German-speaking black wolfsretter trailing as the other drifted away. "You have been traveling in the company of a vampire calling himself Spatar Goran Karahan."

"I cannot deny it."

"Have you some allegiance to him? Owe him some favor?"

"No, and I owe allegiances to no one but my pack and my mate."

Tepes drew to a stop. "But you have no mate."

A keen piece of knowledge for someone he'd just met. Of course, if the wolfsretter could speak to his feelings for Gerwalta, at the very least rumors to that effect might be swirling at court. Only, who would want to speak on such matters, and to what end? They'd only just arrived in Venice. How could the court of the Doge know what Gerwalta's mother did not?

The comment could not have possibly been meant as an offense, but it stunned all the same. "I am courting my intended. It is just a matter of formality."

As in, Gerwalta's eschewing hers.

"My wishes for your joyous mating, then." A few more steps

found them in the lushness of a courtyard, its garden still green in the crisp of the Venetian winter. The craftmenship of the stonework beneath their feet spoke of wealth, and the smoking pots of smoldering incense on the edges perfumed the space with the scent of roses that might have been present had it been summer.

"Why you are here is simple. I wish to employ your services."

"They are not available."

"Ah but wait until you hear my offer." Tepes drew to a stop in the middle of the courtyard. "Tomorrow night is *Carnivale*. A silly tradition, in my opinion, but one observed with some relish here in Venice. The Doge will play host to every vampire who calls this island home, as well as several coming from further ports."

No doubt then the timing of their quest. Whomever these errant blooded sons of Karahan were, they would be at such a celebration.

"Karahan has come a long way to attend." Laughter rumbled in the vampire's chest. "I can see from the raised angle of your brow that you were unaware of this."

"There is no reason for the Spatar to burden me with his affairs."

"No, of course not, but he should have let you know that in the tradition of my kind, he has brought a gift to offer the Doge. Further, he should have told you that *you* are that gift."

Andreas flinched. "I beg your pardon?"

"This year, every bloodline was expected to present the Doge with a lupine. *My father* selected you."

They came from nowhere, but suddenly they were everywhere. Vampires, six in total besides Tepes, flanking his every side. Instinct said to shift, but a silver collar suddenly forced around his throat held him in flesh. His strength betrayed him, and reason fled. Andreas fell to his knees, crying through the pain as the sextet drug him to the side of the courtyard, through a door, past several rooms, and finally into a windowless cell in which sat a silver cage.

Correction: cages. As they tossed him in, the sizzle at his throat eased. Andreas peered out through watering eyes as the last drops of silver returned to their master.

The black hood.

Tepes leaned in. "Are you ready to hear my offer now, Herr Baron?"

The konigswolf glared.

"Good. Tomorrow night, when my father approaches your cage, Mehmet," he motioned to the wolfsretter behind him, "will be watching. He will revoke the silver so that you may escape, at which juncture, you will kill Karahan. When this task is done, I will guarantee your safety out of the city. I will pay you with your still-beating heart."

It took more than the pain of silver to make the kongiswolf turn his back on his principles. "I will not harm someone who has given me no offense."

"Ah, so you're one of those rare lupines with the ability for higher thought—and by virtue of it, like to negotiate."

Tepes leaned in, clutching the bars. "Counteroffer: kill Karahan, and we will let both you *and* your beauitful traveling companion live."

Andreas's blood ran cold. "You will not lay a finger on her."

"Do as I say, and I will not."

With a quick sweep of his head, Andreas took in the sight of the other cages. "And them? Are they under your employ too?"

"No, Herr Baron. They are here as food. You could join them on the menu, if you wish."

A wolf would escape a trap no matter the cost, even if it meant chewing off its own foot. A werewolf was no different. "You promise that Gerwalta will be unharmed?"

"Of course."

"Fine, then." His head hung low. "Agreed."

FOURTEEN

Sleep refused to share her bed, no matter how the wolfsretter lectured herself that she needed the rest. She visualized forms and tactics, remembrances of training she'd done as a girl. Strategy dictated control of the konigswolf, and by proxy, the pack. Divide, isolate, conquer: those were the rules when facing more than one adversary. Surely taking on multiple vampires would be no different. Only, once she knew who they were, she need only divide, isolate, and *capture*. Thank god they were all men and Venetian fashions favored her figure. Only, could she still walk, concealing so much silver under the petticoats she wore?

A knock on her door at sunset roused her from what little sleep she'd managed.

Mazzi's lady's maids were punctual if not brave.

"Come in."

Who entered was no maid. He wasn't a lady.

Violet eyes found her through the darkness. Crimson lips pulled a sinister smile, framing pearlescent fangs. "Fraulein."

Gerwalta sprang from bed, summoning a blade forged in the moment, ready to attack the vampire if he took another step. "I will strike if you attack. I will not be used as a fountain."

If he had any sense of inappropriateness, given that she wore only bedclothes, Massimo did not evidence it. "Dress and join us downstairs immediately." He dropped a swath of clothing on a table near the door.

"You have some nerve, Messer, to barge into my room and make commands of me when last night, your minion had me by the vein." She turned the blade in her hand. "What are you doing here and where is Andreas Baron?"

"They told me you may prove difficult." The vampire grimaced, his rough jaw working. "I have no time to flatter the curiosities of some… some… little red riding hood. Dress with haste and meet us in the dining room. Our time is limited and our mission, critical, if you want to save your wolf."

She shuddered when the door slammed in his wake, though not from the sound or the action. *If you want to save your wolf….* She knew Andreas was in danger, but she refused to acknowledge that he may be in mortal danger. Hadn't Karahan promised it wasn't so? Andreas, dead? Oh, certainly she threatened that it would be the outcome if he didn't cease attempting to make love to her, but *actually* die?

Her heart couldn't take it. If Andreas died then, and she hadn't told him that she loved him….

Gerwalta couldn't let that happen.

Karahan looked up from the flames dancing on the hearth when Massimo entered the dining room, burning twice as hot.

"You insolent, watcher cur!" the Venetian spat. "Is it not bad enough that you involved other dark one lines to clean up your mistake, but you didn't even tell her who you were?"

"She knows who Vlad is now, and that I am his blooded father." Karahan held up his hands. "I admit that I've restricted details on a need-to-know basis. Gerwalta has been hired to accomplish a task, nothing more. She is the means to an end."

"Then her life means nothing to you?" Massimo spat, fetching a tumbler of brandy from the table and pulling it to his lips. "For all your idealism, you're just as selfish as your accursed sons, selectively sharing truths and not caring who your deeds cut down in the process."

Karahan leaned forward in his chair, the definition of serenity. "Where is this spite coming from, Massimo? Where the concern? Could it be that she reminds you of Catalina?"

Rage suffused a voice which grew monstrous in its restraint. "Do not speak her name if you wish to live through this night, Goran or Igor or whatever fallacy you've created yourself as."

Just as the veiled threat was uttered, the wolfsretter entered the dining room, tailed by their host.

"Speak whose name?" Mazzi asked. "If it is Gerwalta Faust, worry no more, for she is here."

Angelo Mazzi was a fool of a slayer. More concerned about warming his bed with new conquests—male or female—than undertaking his sacred duties. If he had, then the rotten branch of the Dracule family tree would have been obliterated when they'd shown up in Venice six months before. Instead, they lingered, corrupting the vampires of a city much too small for so many laity deaths to go unnoticed. Every vampire community dealt with outliers, grifters on the edge of society who risked everyone's discovery with selfish, indecent action. The Ravens brought such behavior into the Doge's Palace, normalizing the irrational.

Massimo was about to bite into the slayer when he turned…

"Fraulein Faust—"

…and found himself dumbstruck.

Yes, she did bare some resemblance to Catalina.

Dedicated as he was to the memory of his deceased wife, the vampire's desires stirred, both for Gerwalta's blood and for her bed. Crimson cloth wrapped around a striking feminine frame. Black skirting in the center of the dress drew the eyes and begged a man of interest to wonder what lie beneath. Golden embellisments suggested buttons, and what did a button long for but to be undone? The Venetian court favored tight bodices, and this dress conformed. A sampling of cleavage where Gerwalta's womanly assets had been wrestled into submission teased the imagination.

And her neck…. Her beautiful, long neck which had already healed from the attack the night before, appeared now as untapped flesh, begging to be breached.

Mazzi grimaced. "Put away those fangs, my sanguineous friends," he said, switching the conversation from Italian to German for Gerwalta's sake. "She is not your breakfast."

Karahan turned to the wolfsretter, mumbling an apology, telling Massimo he had not been alone in his attraction. If even the old Dracule found temptation in this morsel, surely Vlad would want to eat her alive. Anyone who could hold the Bloody Prince's attention stood a chance at bettering.

Massimo retracted his fangs and pushed himself off the wall he'd been leaning against. "Fraulein Faust, I trust in dressing, you came to appreciate its design."

"Its design?" Karahan turned on Massimo. "Other than the fact that it's the precise color of rich blood as it flows from the veins?"

But it was Gerwalta who answered. "Silver has been sown into pockets under the skirt, and several of the elements in the... *supporting features* have also been constructed of it." She ran a hand over one of the bustles jutting from her hip. "Yes, the design is exquisite. It is also far too complex to have been put together since last night." She waited for a response that never came. "Fine, then. Keep your peace. Tell me again what the plan is."

Massimo gave him an admonishing glare before opening into explanations. "When you arrive, locate the seven men wearing raven-shaped masks. That would be Vlad and his generals. In turn, there are to be seven wolves who will be presented tonight at the Doge's palace."

Gerwalta blanched. "And by 'presented,' you mean?"

"As dinner," Karahan said. "We feed off the laity for sustence, but it is known among all vampires that the sweetest blood comes from other dark ones. Rare is it, however, that vampires and wolves find themselves in the same environs. The lupines harvested from each family will be served tonight as a holiday treat."

"But seven lupines together?" Gerwalta said. "Even if they are not a pack, they will function as one when under threat. I am certain a palace full of vampires would win such a confrontation, but no doubt several would be slain in the melee. That would hardly seem the desire of a gracious host."

Massimo clicked his tongue. "The wolves are being housed in silver cages."

The wolfsretter's jaw dropped. "The other wolfsretter. The one from the House of Night...."

"There are two actually," Mazzi said. "But never fear, Fraulein. They are allied with our cause."

"A cause, despite what's been made known to me thus far, that I am still unaware of. But I believe I am beginning to piece it together." She turned to Karahan. "Why do you wish to see the Doge deposed?"

Karahan kept his lips sealed and the truth, close to his heart. To expose it was to open himself to discovery.

Luckily, Massimo found a balance between confidentially and confidence and steered the conversation back unto secure ground. "Because Luciana, put in power in Venice twenty years ago to prevent Tepes's influence spreading, now fosters it. He's injected himself through her affections into the rule of Venice's dark ones. The Ravens already control Istanbul and all the regions which fall under the Ottoman flag. The Bloody Prince wants a war, one that will pit vampires against wolves, and—"

"Yes," Gerwalta cut in, emotions in her voice barely concealed. "That part I know. And since my activities in Nuremberg last year thwarted a plan that would have given rise to lupines among the Holy Roman Emperor's forces...."

"The gateway to the west for the Ottomans is Venice," Massimo said. "Our trade, influence, and location make Venice the perfect garden to plant a seed of discord that will lead straight to Rome, and through Rome, to its armies. Vlad learned the lesson about putting all eggs in one basket. This time, he will use all of the baskets. If all Christendom rises, it will favor his ambitions."

"Then he is a fool. This is no longer the age of Crusades. Europe is not the monolith he thinks it is." She shook her head. "It is not that I do not understand the danger, gentlemen. It's that I don't understand why the solution is merely to contain Tepes and his conspirators instead of kill them?"

Massimo rolled his eyes. "And they say *we* are the blood-thirsty ones?"

"The hoods simply have a different culture," Karahan countered, shooting daggers at the Italian. "She does not know that in our society, bloodlines are more than mere relations."

Mazzi handed the German woman a glass of brandy. "What he means to say, Fraulein, is that there are practical considerations... a system of checks and balances, if you will, that prevent the member of bloodline from destroying any of his or her own. The consequences can be lethal."

She chewed on that a moment before bobbing her head. "Understood. So, then, I have seven vampires to contain. That will call for signifigant amounts of silver. I suppose I am to use the cages then?"

"Indeed. Mehmet and Ahmet, the black hoods, were critical to assuring the supply would be available on site."

This girl.... Her insights were impressive. She'd been trained in strategy. Well-trained.

"The seven wolves are each to their own containment, and as a precaution in case of any breakouts," Massimo continued. "During *Carnivale*, each of the Ravens will be assigned a cage to guard. The Doge will take first choice and first bite. When her fangs strike, all vampire eyes will be on her. That will be your cue to leach the silver from the cages and use it to contain Karahan's damned progeny."

The wolfsretter coughed, or so Massimo thought, until it became clear that she was laughing.

"Something amusing, wolf-killer?"

Her smile sank, her eyes sharpened. "Yes, that clearly none of you understand the nature of my talents," she spat. "Wolfsretters are not slayers. We do not put on grand light shows like that... *thing* that Messer Mazzi did."

"It's called a solarium, Fraulein," the slayer informed her. "It's actually a small flare of sunlight, and—"

Gerwalta waved her hand, cutting him off. "The point is, a wolfsretter's acts are swift, precise, and most importantly, covert. I cannot wield silver that I am either not in contact with or within my line of sight. In a room so crowded, and surrounded by hostile opposition? There is no possible way I can simultaneously warp seven wolf-sized silver cages, let alone use that silver to entrap seven deadly vampires."

The three men exchanged confused glances, as though they had just been informed the very air about them had been laced with poison and weren't certain if they should continue to breathe.

Finally, Massimo threw up his hands. "I told you, Goran, this plan is fantasy. Now thanks to you, I shall never have my revenge."

Karahan batted the air dismissively. "You are a young vampire, Massimo, but surely even your limited two decades of night have taught you that never happens."

"A child's saying, for someone who makes childish plans. This leaves me no choice. I will do what I intended before you filled my head with unicorn visions of a peaceful transfer. I will murder Luciana and send her to sleep in the sea, just like she did to my wife and child."

The old vampire's fangs slashed through his lips. "Do and die."

The Italian's chest backed Karahan into the wall. "I died with Catalina. It is only revenge that lives in me."

Both vampires threw hands over their eyes and hissed as the room blazed.

"Gentlemen, peace." Mazzi's solarium, a ball of death for the warring vampires that he used to regain their civility, cowed both dark ones, forcing them apart.

The wolfsretter stepped between them. "Listen to me, the both of you. Your politics are of concern to me only insofar as my love is now a prisoner because of it. I *will* go to this *Carnivale* to save Andreas, but I will leave you to your revenge and your intrigues."

Karahan slid in front of the retreating wolfsretter, who blinked her surprise. "Are you forgetting, Fraulein, that we have a contract?"

"Your contract is with my mother, not me. Take up your grievance with her."

"And you think your rescue mission will go that smoothly?" Massimo added. "Simply walk into the Doge's palace and walk away with a tribute wolf? As you yourself noted, there will be no end to the number of observers."

"I am amazingly inventive. I'll find a way to free him. And when I do, we will hasten to make our escape."

The slayer, his sympathetic eye falling on the innocent girl, clicked his tongue. "Oh, Fraulein, you forget that Venice is not the forests and fields you are accustomed to. It is an island. Where will you run when you reach the water's edge?"

"Yes, Gerwalta," Karahan said, daring to use her familial name.

"Where *will* you run? Surely not back to Triberg. Even if you do manage to free Herr Baron, as you said yourself, you'll find no safe harbor under the dominion of the House of Red."

Her cheeks blazed the same deep crimson as the color of her gown. "Are you threatening me, *Igor?*"

"I do not mean to threaten, only to remind you that you are in a unique situation. One I could assist you to resolve."

She bit her lip, attempting to hide her fretting. "No, I will accrue no debt in this matter. Besides, where would we go, if not home? Forget the dangers to me, what will become of Andreas's pack if I do not return? No, we.... We will return. I, to wed. He, to lead."

"And your love for one another?" Karahan asked, lifting her chin. "Even if you survive, what of that?"

"What of it? It is impossible. I will convince my mother to force his paw, to arrange for his mating to another wolf, by force if necessary. And I will marry into a foreign line with haste. My would-be assassin only wishes to neutralize my ability to become Matron. I will leave the Schwarzwald by marrying into a foreign bloodline with haste, and Andreas will have a mate and a future."

"Or...."

His sing-songy interjection drew hope into her eyes.

"Or what?"

"Or we make a new contract, one between you and me, and not you and your mother." He pressed her cheeks between his hands. "I am a vampire of particular influence, Gerwalta. If you must marry, perhaps I can assure a *sympathetic* spouse, one that would allow you and Andreas to be mated, while maintaining the public illusion of a proper marriage. The laity royals do it all the time."

"No house would ever accept a wolfsretter being with a wolf."

Massimo, silent this long while, barked a laugh. "You'd be surprised."

"I would?" she asked him before turning back to Karahan.

He withdrew his hands. "Would Andreas stand ready to pass down his command to another wolf and risk moon madness to pursue you? The journey will be long and dangerous."

"I would do the same for him, if I knew it would mean we could be together."

Karahan clapped and rubbed his hands. "Then we will make it so. But you *must* aid in this task. I cannot do it without you. My son and his generals must be stopped, for the sake of all dark ones everywhere. Do this for me, *with me*, and I swear that no harm will come to Andreas, and that after, you will have an opportunity to live your lives together."

In an instant, the wolfsretter threw her hands around his neck and embraced Karahan.

With a firm jaw, she nodded. "If you can swear to this, then I shall find a way."

FIFTEEN

So many lights, so many voices, so many laymen and buildings and dogs running through alleys.

And so, so much water.

Messer Mazzi had been right to mock her plans to escape. How would she and Andreas succeed in fleeing across this? The long, slender boat that served as their coach-upon-the-water moved with enough grace, but she had never learned to swim. The sea between Venice and the mainland made any upon it an easy target for a properly-gifted marksman. Andreas, perhaps, could make it, if he was in any condition to do so when everything was said and done. But with her bustles and corset and petticoats? Her clothing would be her undoing.

And that was before considering the silver she had concealed.

A lick of a wave rocked their boat. Despite sitting, Gerwalta grabbed the edge of the prow for balance.

"Fraulein Faust?" Karahan's hand landed on her shoulder. "Are you all right?"

"I am fine." She righted herself. "Back to proper names, are we?"

The vampire laughed under his breath. "Yes, my apologies for presuming familiarity. I would advise not addressing me as Igor where we're heading."

She turned over her shoulder. "Why is it that you have two names, anyhow?"

"Oh, I have many more than two. A vampire lives a very long time, and by necessity, we must reinvent ourselves now and then. Especially if, like me, one finds himself highly engaged in the world of the laity. Names are like crops, Fraulein. You plant them, nurture them, grow them, reap, then cut them down to their roots until it's time to grow another."

"And just what fruit does Spatar Goran Karahan bear?"

"Goran is a perhaps the only thing preventing my son's efforts to seed the Ottoman forces. I have created the layman persona to use the Sultan's network of spies to my advantage."

"And Igor?"

The vampire's eyes cast out over the water. "Igor is the only thing that will keep it from happening in the future."

The oarsmen continued their labors, rowing them into the heart of Venice. This city…. It toppled on top of itself, a maze of stone and water. How were the captive wolves enduring it? She was more given to laity norms than Andreas, and even she felt the tightness in her chest pulling in.

"Fraulein?" This time it was Mazzi asking after her.

The slayer may be somewhat incorrigible, but he was kind.

"I am not accustomed to boat travel. It gives one a queer feeling of being ill."

"Perhaps you are ill, but it is not from the rocking of the boat." The brotherly Italian grinned. "You have had a tepid pallor about you since you excused yourself at my home to… what was it, pray?"

For a moment she shuddered. Did he somehow know? Could slayers sense silver whereas vampires could not? Even then, how would Messer Mazzi know the silver she concealed had been blood-claimed? Running so much through her heart in so little time almost killed Gerwalta, but she refused to head unprepared into enemy territory where wolfsretters of questionable allegiances dwelled. She would not have sole command of anything the conspirators had put to use in the cages, but she would have rights to what she herself wore.

"Ah, we are here." Karahan stood, the act so smooth, his balance so precise, the boat gave no evidence of motion. "Best to put your masks on then."

The vampire did so even as he suggested it. Gerwalta tried to memorize the features of the alabaster faux face crisscrossed by golden embellishments and capped with a black, triquarter hat. Turning to Mazzi, she realized she'd have a terrible time doing so, for his did not vary from the format in any significant way she'd recall after several moments.

"Fraulein, if you please?"

Gerwalta had no mask, but the trio of conspirators had planned it that way. After all, even though they'd smuggled in enough silver, why miss an opportunity to sneak in a little more?

The wolfsretter fetched a bag tied at her waist and loosed its drawstring. Inside, the silver coins toppled and clicked. In moments, they all obeyed her command, molding themselves into the image she pictured in her head. Irony was not an art in which she was well-rehearsed, but when the mask took the form of a wolf over her face, she earned Messer Mazzi's approval.

Even their arrival to the palace gates was by water. Footmen dressed in the most lavish servants attire she'd ever seen waited at the dock, aiding young maidens such as herself in gracefully sliding onto solid land, likely also assuring the guests that were disembarking were of the appropriate species, or at the very least, escorted appropriately. It only took a few steps into the entry courtyard for the whispers to die away and for fangs to show.

They wanted her, but which part of her? Her blood or her body? Both, likely. Perhaps the wolfsretter were animal enough to sense such things, for Gerwalta could not eschew the hungry glances coming her way. Nor could she dismiss the tingling in her fingertips and lurch in her stomach when she sensed the wolves. Seven distinct energies, just as she'd been advised there would be. Five were roughly the same to her, their taste feral and pure. One held a distinct ambiance of the familial. That would be Andreas, no doubt, and her heart lifted at the thought that he might sense her too and know his confinement was to end.

The seventh.... The seventh was something she'd never encountered before. Wolf, but a *different* kind of wolf. Temptation gripped her, but would she have opportunity to assuage it and do what she needed to?

"I feel like a cut of meat being dangled before dogs," she whispered into Karahan's ear. "Can they all tell so easily that I am potential food?"

"The heartbeat does give you away, I'm afraid." The elder vampire led her toward the entry to the house proper. "It is an advantage. Massimo knew what he was doing when he presented you that gown. Most vampires can be manipulated by good, old-fashioned lust."

She stopped, pivoting toward him. "Can you?"

He pulled her hand to his lips, his mask cut in such a fashion as to show his mouth. Most around were; no doubt a vampire would demand a way to display his ivory trophies.

"I have learned my lesson about indulging the flesh. The fang is a cruel master and an unforgiving a teacher. But you do tempt me to forget my learning."

"Well, if it isn't Papa Dracule himself."

They turned to find a stout man of perhaps fifty years wearing a mask molded to represent the face of the moon.

If irony is in fashion here, Gerwalta thought, *then no doubt this is a slayer.*

"Helsinger." Karahan dropped Gerwalta's hand and beared his fangs. Despite a terrible image, he kept his voice soft. "What are you doing here?"

Helsinger tipped the rim of a black hat ornamented with golden baubbles and bright blue feathers. "I would assume, the same as you."

A growl rumbled through Karahan's chest. Gerwalta blinked away her confusion. Who knew vampires growled?

"Harm anyone of my bloodline and the consequences would be dire."

"I assure you… Spatar Karahan, I'm told you're going by these days, is it? Is that the persona you keep in your Society of Watchers?"

It was bait that Karahan left unnibbled.

"In any event," Helsinger continued with a twirl of his hand, "do you really expect that I can allow your sons' tyranny to continue? Three laymen deaths this week alone, the bodies drained of all blood and left in the canals to feed the fishes. Either they will answer for it, or the Doge…"

"*None* of my bloodline!" Karahan hissed, stepping into the

slayer. "I am resolving the situation tonight. All you need do is stay out of my way."

At this juncture, they were joined by Messer Mazzi. The Italian slayer didn't brandish a solarium—would that have any effect on another slayer, she wondered—but he did produce a rather intimidating dagger from under one sleeve which he took to Helsinger's side shield under his cape.

"Helsinger," Mazzi said. "I would hate to think you're here to encroach on my territory."

"Only insofar as pursuing hostiles from my own, Mazzi."

Karahan's lip curled. "Go back to Budapest, Frederick. I am already busy cleaning up this mess because of your foolish father. I do not want you here causing any more."

Helsinger lunged. Mazzi pulled. Suddenly, Gerwalta had her blade at the interloper's throat. The vampire mass thronged nearby stilled, partaking of the unexpected entertainment with undivided attention.

Helsinger signaled his surrender, hands at the level of his eyes. "Peace, then. I may fight vampires, but I will not fight one of my own. Nor would I dare to take up arms against a woman."

Gerwalta's upper lip curled. "It is good to find a man who recognizes his limits."

And with that, Helsinger withdrew, making for the docks as Karahan took the wolfsretter by the arm and lead her inside, beaming nearly as brightly as Mazzi's solarium.

The vampire took her arm, escorting her in, as she pulled her silver back from sight. "Very impressive."

"I didn't do it to impress you. We have a bargain, one you cannot uphold if you are dead." She shifted her massive dressings around a shrubbery in a stout ceramic pot. "He called you a watcher. A watcher of what?"

Karahan shrugged. "People, times, events. We are a loose network of vampires who attempt to chronicle the major shifts in dark one culture, to document and to preserve."

"To what end?"

"Why, to find a cure, of course."

She stopped, looked at him askew. "Are you ill?"

"We all are, in a manner of speaking. All dark ones are at least partially human. If we were not, we could not reproduce with the laity."

The very thought of such a coupling made her face screw up.

"I merely speak of *possibility*, not a preference," he said. He took her arm and encouraged her to continued. "Helsinger thinks we have sinister plans afoot, however, and that we are somehow looking for secrets and weaknesses with which to exploit all creatures. Given that the only Watcher he knows is me, and that my bloodline is guilty as charged, I cannot entirely fault his conclusion."

"Perhaps, but you certainly do not seem like you're trying to exploit anyone."

A cloud overcame his features. "If only you knew, Fraulein."

SIXTEEN

Andreas eyeballed the silver cage before him. He couldn't put it off any longer; he'd need to get in. The black-cloaked wolfsretter who'd brought him to Venice, Mehmet, had shaped it in such a way as to allow ample width for arms to be pulled through without touching, but that was only if the vampires who sought to drink from him were careful not to tug and pull.

"What do I do if they drink too much before Karahan approaches?" the lupine asked. "If I am too weak to attack...."

Tepes clicked his tongue. "I have told the Doge that I will guard the cage with the wolf who will kill Karahan. Only she will take your vein. That very act will draw Karahan forward. He'll attempt to talk her out of it. He still believes he can bend her ear."

The konigswolf raised an eyebrow. "Can he?"

The Bloody Prince's eyes wandered to the right. "Surely you don't believe yours is the only aid I've sought tonight."

Andreas saw the threads of the weave. "Another wolf will target the Doge if she refuses to act her part."

"But she does not know which one. No one does, except the wolf and I." The vampire clapped Andreas on the shoulder. "It is time, Herr Baron. Do as I say, and I will see to it that your beloved survives tonight. Fail, and.... Well, I've always been curious about the taste of red hood. I hear they are quite sweet, from the vein and... in *other* places."

Before the konigswolf could mount a proper retort—something in the way of ripping the vampire's throat out, Tepes was a cloud of smoke drifting over the floor. So stunned was he by the feat that when the Turkish wolfsretter approached him from behind, he did not notice.

"Do not give the bloodsucker the honor of your anger," Mehmet said. "He does not respect women. He either drinks them or beds them to the point of death, then tosses their bodies aside, used and forgotten. Such a man deserves neither time nor consideration."

Forcing loose his fists, Andreas turned. "That does not mean he does not pose a great threat."

Mehmet grimaced. "For now."

The konigswolf's head tilted like that of a curious pup. "Meaning?"

"It will become clear when it becomes clear."

Mehmet motioned toward the one cage that remained unfilled and flicked his fingers. Silver bars became liquid metal, pooling in waves left and right, until a door manifested.

Andreas stepped in, careful that none of his flesh contacted the corrosive structure. "Will the other wolves all be permitted to go free?"

"It is not my concern."

"So the House of Night is not so different from the House of Red."

A loose motion of Mehmet's hands, and the bars of the cage reformed. "I do not speak Italian, and that is all most of the wolves know. It is possible they have struck some deal with the vampires; they are not in the habit of making their plans known to me. The only agreement I am party to is for the release of the shewolf."

"The shewolf? Why? What is she to you?"

The wolfsretter clenched his jaw and turned away.

"Oh, come now," Andreas said. "If all goes as planned, you will head east and I will run north. We are never to see each other again."

"But you might carry the knowledge, and that could cost her her life. Do not ask for a dagger from my hand and say you have no mal intentions. It would not matter; the blade was made to rend."

At that, Andreas cut off his query. "Then let us turn to more practical matters. Karahan: Does he have allies in the crowd that will come to his aid?"

"Two of note, one being he in whose home you were being hosted."

Mazzi made sense, of course. No doubt a vampire with a slayer at his back would not be trifled with easily. But in a palace full of vampires?

"The other?"

"He will reveal himself if he deems it appropriate."

"And that is all? Two allies, one who may remain in the shadows, taking on seven who have the backing of the Doge of Venice?" Andreas's head shook. "Do you think me a fool, Mehmet?"

"No, Andreas, I do not." The corner of the wolfsretter's mouth lifted as he ran a hand over the silver bars. "The most dangerous weapon is that which is invisible to the eye while in plain view. The most powerful warrior, one who is underestimated."

Tepes has no respect for women.

Among the wolfsretter, women were the dominant sex. Stronger, faster, able to work silver with an ease that left their male counterparts dizzy. Mehmet had managed to construct cages with the materials he'd been provided.

Gerwalta could build a whole prison.

A wolf feared silver, but Andreas found a new-born respect for his trappings. "It must take a tremendous amount of silver to contain a wolf. I wonder if it would be enough to contain a vampire?"

"An interesting question." Mehmet nodded. "I am not a slayer. It is not my place to speculate on such topics."

Andreas grinned. "No, you'd need a vampire of some wisdom to determine that course of action, as well as a warrior capable of achieving such a feat."

"Indeed, Herr Baron. And where would one find such a warrior in Venice?"

"One wouldn't."

Mehmet gave Andreas a slow nod before leaving in the direction of the courtyard.

SEVENTEEN

They stood like garrisons protecting the castle. Only, instead of being placed on the towers facing out, each of the six raven-masked men she'd identified stood at one of the pillars that supported the floors of the palace.

Trying to keep people out or hold people in? she wondered as she wove through the crowd.

The pull of the wolves proved stronger on the west half of the courtyard, but she could do nothing about that now. Gerwalta tried to stay focused, reminding herself that when the opportunity came, she must endeavor to trap the vampires she'd been hired to stop, not strive solely to save Andreas. If she did the first, it would accomplish the latter. If Karahan was a man of his word, he would take them to a land where they could find refuge. To a land where they could be together.

Her body shivered. Not from the chill in the air, but from the thought that in a very short time, she'd find a wolf in her bed. Their last encounter had nearly undone her resolve. Gerwalta could no longer talk herself out of the truth; she loved him. Yes, she could do as expected, return to Triberg, become a chess piece for her mother to position with just the right mate, but the thought of being with a man besides Andreas sickened her.

She'd resisted because she knew giving in to her emotions would be the same as signing his execution papers. Now, if she managed to complete this task, there was a way for them to be together.

Even if it did mean she'd give up her family and their homeland in the process…

Once more, she scanned the courtyard, straining to find the seventh raven mask that had yet alluded her. The first six had been easy enough to find. But now, as she took in the visions of fish and fowl, jesters and dukes, lords and ladies, her quest was fruitless.

Suddenly, the hairs on the back of her neck stood to attention.

Someone was behind her. No, he was veritably against her back, his words tickling her neck as he spoke lowly in the court language.

"I am afraid that I do not speak Italian. Do you, perchance, know German?"

"Fraulein, my German, like my touch, is as smooth as silk." He laughed, his lips pressed against her ear. "And what I said was, 'Is your mask any implication of your preference for bed sport?'"

Where there had been fascination, fury burned. Gerwalta spun, ready to dig her heels into the throat of the brash vampire when she froze.

A beak.

The last raven presented fangs for her approval. No matter the inappropriateness of his speech, she knew she could not risk it. Gerwalta was an expert hunter; few laymen could compete. She knew an elusive animal when she saw one. If she let this vampire from her sight, he could fly away.

A sweep of the room confirmed the others' unchanged positions. Gerwalta wove her arm through his. Karahan himself had told her she'd been dressed to be a feast to the eyes. Now she needed to suggest to the vampire there may be other parts of her he could feed upon. How wondrous a thing that the male of all species could be so easily misled by vanities. *It can be a powerful tactic in some situations,* she remembered being told when younger and still training. *Arousal draws blood away from the head in men, slows their thinking.*

Though she did have to wonder: as vampires had no pulse, did their blood draw anywhere?

"If you mean, do I favor lupines over vampires, I must admit my ignorance. I have never partaken of either."

"Ah, only your kind, then."

Her movements jolted, even as they bowed before joining the other dancers already swirling about. "My own kind?"

"I hear your heartbeat, Fraulein. I know you are a layman."

Play up his misconception. "You have found me out, Herr…?"

The dance demanded that he take her hand at that point, but

Gerwalta had a feeling he would have done so anyway.

"Tepes. *Vlad* Tepes."

Her blood turned to ice as she pulled her hand back.

"You know of me." Amusement pulled at the corners of his mouth.

She nodded. "The Bloody Prince."

"And here I thought the laity called me only The Impaler."

Gerwalta's heart pounded. Was that true? Did she just give away that she was not, in fact, of the laity?

"There is no call to fear me, Fraulein. Though, if you do not slow that heart of yours, others of my kind might be tempted to challenge me for your attention."

The wolfsretter inwardly lectured herself on the heels of such sage advice. Why was she fretting so? Was it because her body, though outwardly healed of the wound, still recalled the pierce of fangs just the night before? But then she'd been unprepared. Surely a wolfsretter could stand her ground against a single vampire, if not ambushed. They had the advantage of speed, no doubt, but her strength did not suffer compared to theirs.

The night air vibrated as the first strike of midnight carried from the tower dominating the islands. If what Massimo had said was true, the lupines would soon be revealed to the audience. Even in her peripheral vision, her targets began to shift position, collapsing in on a set of double doors on the east side of the courtyard, the same place she had sensed the wolves.

It had been her body that attracted him. Perhaps it could keep him there as well.

"Is it only my *heart* that would draw them?" Gerwalta eschewed her fear and bolstered her courage. With a lithe finger, she traced an invisible line down her neck, being certain to draw attention to the thick vein showing through her pale skin. "Is that all that interests vampires?"

Vlad followed that finger with alarming focus. The vampire licked his lips. "Are you asking about my kind as a whole, or me specifically?"

Her own words sickened her. "Perhaps I am asking if you could give me a demonstration of your *impaling* prowess."

His fangs gleamed, twin daggers hungering for flesh. A few nearby vampires had slowed their dancing, watching.

Vlad stepped forward, embracing her head in both his hands. "Tell me your name, so I know what to scream when I pour myself inside you."

On the east side of the courtyard, there was movement. Seven large carts, covered over with curtains so the contents remained hidden from view, drew squeaks from the wheels beneath. One by one they were lined up on the edge where the revealers were gathered. Three to the north end, three to the south end, each flanked by one of Vlad's men. Purpose called to her when the wolfsretter who'd defended her attacker the night before pushed out the last cart without aid. If Massimo Brunelli could be believed, this man was one of Karahan's coconspirators. It was good to see his physical strength proved great.

Vlad turned back to her. "Stay, have fun. But if any other tries to claim you, tell them you belong to the prince. As soon as this concludes, you will join me in my apartment in the palace."

She feigned anticipation, licking her lips and rolling up on her toes. "Yes, your Highness."

He leaned in, grabbing her chin. "And be certain to eat well."

"I do not understand." All said and done, that was a curious request.

"You shall need a great deal of strength to last through what I have planned for you." He leaned in, raking a fang across her lips. *Nipped it*. No blood, the action was only meant to play.

Or promise.

Or threaten.

"As soon as I can return, I shall."

Gerwalta waited a few moments before following. What a fortunate encounter. She'd written herself an excuse to be at the front of the assembly when the wolves were revealed. None would question her trying to stay in the line of sight of her potential paramour.

She began to make her way across the room when, on the north end of the courtyard, there was a tremendous crash.

EIGHTEEN

The Doge loved being adored. She adored being loved. Almost as much as she loved being feared.

Both of her fathers had spoiled her. The human one raised a pampered princess, and her father-of-the-blood consigned her beauty to the shelter of immortality. Even the voluminous, Venetian fashions could not blanket her many curves, and her handsome face and ebony hair tied in elaborate knots and swells made her an adventure that must be taken to be believed.

Massimo hated to admit he *had* taken it, but never from a place of true desire. It had been a means to an end, a way to get close to power. He knew better than to expect that he could rid his glorious city and republic of its vampire menace. By becoming one of them, and then finding a way to rule them, he could, perhaps, keep what had happened to him from happening to anyone else.

Now, victory was within his grasp, and winning all depended on the abilities of a single woman from a foreign land with questionable intentions. A wolfsretter, nonetheless. But could she really accomplish the mission? If Tepes and his generals were again contained, the Doge would lose her base of power. If the Doge lost her base of power, Massimo could rise against her. If he rose against her, and if enough of the vampires of Venice backed his claim, he would control the city.

Massimo flinched at the sound of the cymbals crashing. Schooling his features, he turned and carried out his role, taking to the Doge's side as her second.

"I welcome the noble families," the Doge began, holding out her hands. "You have come from all over the countryside, even from foreign shores, to join my celebration tonight. Across town, the mortals drink their wine and sing their celebrations. We let them, untouched. Untouched, for tonight, we dine not on the Venetian people, but on the tributes presented to our great republic by the seven families themselves. Tonight, we dine on… the blood of the lupines!"

A flourish of the Doge's hand was the signal for the raven-masked vampires on the east side of the courtyard to pull the coverings from the cages. Massimo averted his eyes. He did not care for lupines as a species per se, but they were also men, and he did not care to see any subjugated simply because of the creature god had made him.

Even if one of the wolves was a woman.

The slide of the Doge's hand into his own pulled open his eyes.

Luciana gazed on him with tenderness in plain view. "Why do you hide your eyes, my love?"

A moment he allowed for the disgust to boil within before shoving it away. He took on his role: the dutiful lover, the supporting right-hand man.

Massimo pulled the Doge's hand to his lips, kissing her knuckles. "I do not hide my gaze, I save it for your beauty."

She beamed. "As it should be."

He spoiled her rotten, because *that's* what Luciana expected. And the moment her lovers grew tired of sating her every need, she had them executed.

Or she ran back to one of her fathers. They took turns placating her need for constant affirmation. He expected no less of Vlad Tepes—Luciana's weakness gave him power over her, and detest Luciana though Masimo did, he did not discredit her power. Of course, she was powerful. She was a Dracule. But Igor… or Goran, as he was going by now…. The paterfamilias of his bloodline seemed both mighty and kind, balancing horror and humanity the way few vampires could. How, then, had he come to father so many disappointing children?

"Come." Luciana pulled him from his reverie and insistently toward the courtyard. "I will have first blood, as is my right, but you shall have second, my gift for my beloved consort."

"I have no desire for the werewolf blood." Massimo detested his dependence on laymen blood; drinking that of another dark one, however, felt too much like cannabilism.

"It is not about the *blood*," Luciana said. "It is that you demand it, and by receiving it, you grow powerful in the eyes of the community. Or do you not wish that they should fear you as they do me?"

They do not fear you, he thought. *They fear your fathers.* If there was one pity he felt for his lover-of-convenience, it was that she authentically did not understand she was a puppet ruler. Through his own tyranny, the Wallachian Prince had seized the power of the east, and through proxy and via Venice, soon he would have power over the west as well.

Unless Karahan's plan worked, that was.

Massimo took a breath, summoned a faux face of reverence, and followed in Luciana's wake.

Hopefully, for the last time.

NINETEEN

Andreas's brown eyes held an odd mix of reverence and fear. The reverence, from his love for her. But the fear? Wherefore the fear? She was a wolfsretter surrounded by vast resources of her most agile weapon. Even if she were to be attacked, Gerwalta could draw the silver from the cages to cocoon herself. For a short time, anyhow. Eventually, she would need to breathe.

But when Andreas's gaze drifted, she knew something more than generalized anxiety weighed on him. Was it anxiety? Did he believe she would allow him to become some hellwhore's food?

A line broke through the crowd as the Doge promenaded through the courtyard, the menagerie of masks in the shape of every animal pivoted in her wake. Gerwalta turned when she sensed the movements behind her, and found, much to her surprise, the Doge's consort and his familiar face.

Massimo caught her eye for the briefest of moments as he and the Doge walked past, the warning as clear as though he'd spoken the words aloud. *Do not give me away. Stay with the plan. Be ready to move, the moment is coming.*

Gerwalta's hands tightened into fists, her nails embedding into the heel of her palm. She longed to call the silver; all seven ravens were within view.

"A hair's breadth of difference can keep the axeman's blade from hitting its target."

Beside her, Karahan appeared as if by magic. How could he move so soundlessly?

"Where did you—"

He cut her off with some urgency. "You met Vlad."

A statement, not a query. Had Karahan been spying on her the whole time? Because of concern for her, or the plan?

Gerwalta swallowed down her fear when she realized the Bloody Prince himself caught sight of them talking. Just like that, where Karahan had been, now only air. She met his scowl with haste, mouthing the words, *I am yours.* Her inner wolfsretter rebelled at the act. She was no man's property to claim, and none had rights over her except he whom she permitted to claim her.

And that would only be Andreas. Thoughts of the lupine drew her concern, and she looked up to discover a very curious thing: frustration being thrown her way. Because another stood beside her when he could not? Because he longed for her? No, Andreas's eyes were not, in fact, looking at *her.* They were looking at the space *beside* her, to where Karahan had just been. But why would Andreas be frustrated by Karahan's disappearance? If he was jealous, he'd be glad of it.

Something was very wrong with this whole picture.

The Doge, a misty-skinned beauty with a complex of black hair atop her head, let go Massimo's hand and addressed Vlad. The words, all in Italian, had little meaning to Gerwalta, who only recognized "who" from its likeness to French. It didn't matter; she'd been through enough formal ceremony and pomp to recognize it for what it was. The Doge posed a question, then looked out across the assemblage, as though confirming that her due diligence in the exchange had been executed.

The wolves in the cages, despite residing in their lay forms, began to pace. Predators sensed when they became prey. Vlad returned some equally-rehearsed words before reaching through the cage and taking Andreas by the hand.

She turned, taking one last furtive survey, hoping to find Karahan mixed in with the crowd but ready to back her up if anyone attacked. Her hopes sank as Messer Mazzi's eyes met hers and he shook his head lowly.

Only then did the crowd gasp.

The wolfsretter spun, discovering the Doge, Andreas's arm at her lips, but Karahan's hand on her chest, pushing her away.

"Enough, Inga."

Inga? The Doge of the Venetian court was named Inga?

But there was no time to pause and consider. Already, Gerwalta had missed her cue. She swept her gaze right, then left, checking her line of sight and her targets. The Ravens had come out from their posts a step or two, but they maintained their positions. That wouldn't last, given the scowl erupting across Vlad Tepes's face. A confrontation was emerging, and she had only moments before it was too late.

The wolfsretter focused her mind, called on her power, and beckoned the silver cages up and down the courtyard to obey her will.

And obey they did, shifting shape, bending, melding, becoming liquid streams in the air. But as they began to coalesce into pools of metal, Gerwalta came to a startling realization.

The silver was obeying.

It just wasn't obeying *her*.

And that was when Andreas pounced, knocking Karahan to the ground.

TWENTY

A spark landed in a bed of kindling, the room erputed into flame.

Royal courts were inherently violent places. The only difference between normal discourse and the cacpohny of battle around her was that the weapons in the former were words and here, fangs and claw.

For once, being an outsider brought an advantage; none had issue with her, therefore no reason to seek out and attack when the opportunity presented itself. All around her, vampires squared off, wolves freed from their prisons took their fur, forming a de facto pack intent on making way through the throng to freedom. Except for Andreas, strewn atop Karahan, attempting to chomp at the vampire who'd hired them, and the sole shewolf, who was… being flanked by the two wolfsretters from the House of Night? Was that their role here? Who was this grey-eyed shewolf to demand such consideration?

But Gerwalta couldn't concern herself with contrary behavior. She had to get Andreas off Karahan before the konigswolf destroyed the one man who may be able to deliver them to freedom.

"Andreas!" Gerwalta threw her arms around the wolf from behind, attempting to drag him off. Strong though she was, the mere fact that he outweighed her by a hefty sum made the feat challenging. "He is going to help—"

Karahan, though pinned, held Andreas's drooling maw in his hands and turned toward the wolfsretter. "Don't worry about me!"

"But Andreas will kill you if—"

Karahan met her eyes. "Do it before the opportunity escapes. Get them. My promise remains."

The one he made not to hurt Andreas, to aid them in escaping to someplace where they could have a life together.

She turned back to find the Ravens scattered. Three of them

were stalked toward the edge of the courtyard, where three of the wolves had come together to close in on the Doge. Three wolves might be able to take on one vampire, but four vampires against three wolves would be a lupine blood bath.

Gerwalta had to stop them. At the same time, she knew that if she took down only part of the Ravens' number, the others would flee. Then they would all come for her and, if he lived, Andreas. She and her wolf would be on the run until the end of their days.

Never settling....

Never having an opportunity to start a family....

Gerwalta pushed away the warmth that overcame her at the thought. Now was not the time to dream of domestic bliss. She had to stop the three vampires closing in on the Doge, find the four others in the crowd, and do so with a line of sight to the silver, a line of sight now cluttered by a throng of spatting vampires.

There was only one way to do all that, but the ramifications....

She passed one more longing glance at Andreas at the same moment a vicelike grip took her shoulder.

"So, you're part of this, then?" Tepes growled. "When I'm done with you, you'll wish you were.... Your.... Your eyes. You're a..."

She knew what he must see; the evidence of letting her powers embrace her in full, of calling upon every measure of strength she had. Her eyes would be pools of silver now.

His grip loosened as her feet left ground, but shock cemented him to the spot. The Bloody Prince became small in her eyes as she rose into the air, called upon the seven pillars of silver, and began to embalm the vampires who stood between her and whatever came next.

Until Tepes turned on Andreas, that was.

TWENTY-ONE

He wished Gerwalta could sense his emotions the way another wolf could have. Then she would know how much he loved her, and how sorry he was for what he was about to do.

The moment the cage melted into a pillar beneath his feet, Andreas took his fur, the transformation of his features rending every stitch of the decadent clothing forced upon him into shreds. Only the highly polished heeled shoes remained behind without injury as the lupine leapt. The konigswolf embraced the animal within, leaving his humanity by the wayside. Only then could he have a future with Gerwalta. Only by living up to his side of the bargain and destroying Karahan could she survive to be his bride.

But the vampire under his paws showed strength beyond measure, not to mention patience. Karahan showed no interest in turning the tide. His only intent seemed to be in drawing a stalemate, holding Andreas's open jaws just inches from his throat with such ease, the wolf knew the vampire could throw him off if he really wanted to.

"Whatever you've been told about me is a lie. I intend neither you nor Fraulein Faust any harm."

That might work to disengage the lupine, if that was the basis of his attack—a fact that Karahan seemed to grasp intrinsically when the assault only intensified.

The first crack in Karahan's strength came in the form of a strained expression. "I will not allow them to hurt her either, but I can only do that if you remove yourself from me. The plan remains; she will end them. She will—"

But just then, something changed in the vampire's expression. Karahan's grip slackened, and the sudden shift confused Andreas enough to forestall his taking advantage. The Spatar's eyes fixed over the konigswolf's back, up in the air. A lupine was no cat, but curiousity snatched at Andreas all the same. He took his eyes off the man he was meant to kill and turned, following his gaze.

The moment he saw it, he knew any benefit to killing Karahan was gone. Gerwalta's form floated aloft, as high as the balconies jutting out from the second floor. She was flying in plain view of vampires, slayers, lupines, and worst yet, her own kind. The fact that two wolfsretters from the House of Night played witness would be immaterial, however. An event such as this? It could not be covered as easily as it had been in Nuremberg. News would reach Triberg, and when it did, it would change Gerwalta's life forever. There was nowhere they could run now that the House of Red would not pursue. A wolfsretter's ability to fly was practically a divine sign that such a woman was destined to be Matron. They'd force Gerwalta into the role, under threat of death if needed.

Or if they discovered her love for him, threat of *Andreas's* death.

"Let me up and I can protect her."

Andreas snapped back to the moment. *Not from the real threat. No one can.*

His paws pulled back. The corded muscles of his canine frame relaxed. He was not giving in to Karahan's request; he was letting go the fight. The moment Gerwalta's feet had left the ground, he'd lost her. The will to fight for anything, even himself, deserted him… for what was the purpose of living, if he could not be with the woman he loved?

No sooner had one vampire crawled out from beneath him than another tackled him from behind, viciously strong hands wrapping around his throat.

"You were supposed to kill him!" Tepes growled. "You damned, dirty dog!"

His body fought to endure, even as his heart sank. *Let him kill me,* Andreas told himself. *Better die in battle than alone or having gone mad.*

But Fate had not finished mocking Fortune. Gerwalta's silver-plated eyes peered down, catching the calamity beneath her. Suddenly, she let go her ascent, landing in a lithe crouch just behind them.

The wolfsretter pulled at the store of metal that had been Andreas's cage and made of it a mace, a silver stick topped with spiked globe. In one mighty swing, she walloped the unprepared Bloody Prince upside the head, throwing off his balance and allowing the air to come rushing back into Andreas's lungs.

Beside Andreas on the courtyard stones, Tepes rolled over just in time to find the wolfsretter and her fearsome weapon preparing another blow.

"If you wish to live," Gerwalta bellowed, "leave my mate alone!"

His heart seized, then pounded so hard it made his head spin. Mate? *Mate?* Had she just…. Did Gerwalta just declare that…?

No time to dwell. The moment Tepes got his bearings back, he was on her.

Locked in a struggle for power, neither warrior realized that all around quarreling had ceased to play witness to theirs. Even the wolves turned snouts in their direction. Except for Andreas, whose maw captured Tepes at the ankle, jerking him back. A vile essence coated the konigswolf's tongue, the taste of flesh and blood that had turned stale and rotting.

Tepes shrieked, his suffering feeding Andreas's animal nature. The lupine's jaw tightened, driving sharp fangs into the meat of the vampire's calf. Deeper, deeper, seeking bone, seeking destruction….

You will not take my mate from me. You will not claim what is mine. I will have her; I will destroy you to win.

Such thoughts…. He loved Gerwalta, this he'd understood for months. But what he felt now…. It was more than love, it was…

The beginning of the end. The process which would end in their union, *could only* end with their union, had begun.

Mottled voices flowed in the air around him, but saying what? Andreas did not know. He could focus only on destroying that which threatened to come between them. But to what end? They could not be together, not now.

Only when the silver licked his flesh, driving slices into his front legs, did the hold break. Andreas's mouth released the vampire as pain drove him away. He looked up, blinking away his confusion, to find the source of his torment.

Gerwalta's eyes held the sadness of the world as her hand curled, commanding the silver under her power, burning into his flesh.

She didn't need to say the words for him to know the truth.

It was a reminder, one she was loath to give, but it was critical that he receive.

Yes, they loved each other, but that did not mean they ceased being enemies. The pain reminded him of the one fact that would never change between them.

We are each other's death.

TWENTY-TWO

Gerwalta felt his pain as though she had forced it upon her own person. More than the physical, she also suffered the betrayal, the shock in his eyes. *How could you love me and do this to me?* But what else could she do? She'd wrapped five of the Ravens in silver, forced their bodies to smoke by collapsing them into urns no larger in height or width than her arm. She'd been on the cusp of securing a sixth when she'd noticed Tepes attacking Andreas. *Cut off the head, and the limbs will falter.* It was a truism of warfare, and that was what this had become: warfare. It only made sense then, to shift her focus to the Bloody Prince, forcing number six to collapse with such haste, she couldn't be certain if he'd survive it.

But when Andreas had caught Tepes by the leg and refused to let go, her task proved impossible. Forcibly wrap him in silver, and she'd likely take out half of Andreas's snout in the process.

She'd still love him if he had no nose, of course, but would she ever forgive herself if she was the cause of his injury? A konigswolf must be strong, be able to wield power and demand respect. What did she care if he was not physically perfect as long as he was alive? But the pack might not look upon deformity the same way, and she would not assume his permission when death might be the easier risk to tempt.

The only solution was to use the silver under her command to shock Andreas and loosen his grip.

She hadn't anticipated the other wolves taking advantage of the confusion to attack. In going after one of their own kind, Gerwalta had given the de facto pack a common enemy. They fell in from all sides, teeth bared, maws bloodied from battle. And behind the shewolf, who approached from her left, stalked the two wolfsretters of the House of Night. What? They were siding with the wolves? They were allowing themselves to be led into battle by a shewolf?

What followed all unfolded too fast to comprehend clearly and took her thought elsewhere.

Andreas let go his grip as Karahan's arms encircled him.

Crushing his ribs, perhaps? She'd have to worry about that later. First, he needed to live. Suddenly, Tepes was free of Andreas's hold. Gerwalta forced the only silver she could wield with the encircling pack into submission. The boosted features of her gown went limp as she leached away the blood-claimed silver and forced it to ink over the Bloody Prince's frame.

"I am not a wolf, Fraulein. This will do nothing to—"

His words cut off as the silver began to compress. Vlad held up his hands, the shiny coating making his eyes go wide, as Gerwalta pulled the water-thin layers tighter, tighter, pushing the vampire's form into submission.

From her right, a wolf leapt. Massimo solidified in a black cloud of smoke just in time to catch him midair, a hair's width from his teeth sinking into her arm.

"Hurry, Fraulein!" he shouted, wrestling the beast away. "Stop Vlad!"

Would the other wolves stay focused on her, or attempt to help their fallen comrade? Gerwalta could not wait to see, and if it was indeed her, she could waste no time. Not in trapping Tepes, not in tipping her heart to the man she loved.

"Andreas…"

Silver fingers crushed in on the vampire, running veins up his neck, through his hair.

"I…"

It encircled the prince's neck, slashing flesh.

"…love…"

Tepes, desperately realizing what was going on, thrashed. Left, right, left, right… but the silver refused to slacken.

"…you."

A wolf's maw caught her at the wrist just as her last flourish did the necessary, leaving in the place of the prince, a tall, silver urn. The raven-shaped mask fell to the floor at Gerwalta's feet, along with precious drops of her blood.

The wolf bit hard, likely an effort to sever her hand from her arm. Agony took Gerwalta to her knees, and pain diverted her from the pulses of instinct to fight back. Only a moment later, when hot crimson rivelets splashed to the stones below, did she seek to find some source of silver.

Only suddenly, the pressure lifted.

Gerwalta looked up and found the man she loved, taken again of flesh, holding the wolf who attacked her by the scruff so high in the air, the poor creature's feet scrambled to touch ground.

Gone was the fur, but the animal still colored his voice. "If you hurt my mate again, I will have your pelt for my bed clothes."

Did the captured wolf speak German? Perhaps. It did not seem to matter. The way it pulled in on itself, letting out a high-pitched keen and folding its ears back, signaled submission. With a gruff grunt, Andreas threw the creature to the ground. The wolf whimpered, coming back into his layman form, and promptly running from the courtyard. Thanks be to heaven, none pursued, though whether due to distraction or an actual lack of temptation to sample the blood of lupine, Gerwalta knew not.

As soon as it was from sight, the konigswolf collapsed on the ground beside her, running fingers through her hair, pulling her head to his shoulder. "They promised.... They promised me if I killed Karahan, they would keep you from harm."

The lover's reunion ended as the Doge fumed into their midst.

Andreas shielded Gerwalta with his body, though the dark-haired beauty's fury focused squarely on Karahan.

"How *dare* you?" she demanded, her slender, gloved finger prodding the other vampire's chest. "How *dare you*! This is not Wallachia! Here, I rule. Here, I decide who—"

The blade burst through her front, spackling blood across both Gerwalta and Andreas's faces.

Karahan growled, long, frightening fangs dropping into existence as he moved to the Doge with speeds so daunting, it hurt to turn one's head in time.

The Spatar had Massimo on the floor in a blink, the Italian's face to the ground, Karahan's fangs hovering over his spine.

"We agreed she would not be hurt!"

Despite his position, Massimo did not falter. "We agreed she would not die!" he said. "I have not killed her, even though it is my right."

"You cut through her gullet!" Karahan snapped, lifting, then slamming Massimo's head down. "It will take her a week to heal from such an injury!"

"Then let her heal far from Venice." The Italian turned his head, spit out a mouthful of blood. "Only take her far from me."

"And leave you Doge?"

"And leave me to *grieve*. Properly, without having to lick her boots and flatter her fallacies. Take her and go!"

Gerwalta, fighting the dizziness, looked to the Doge and found what she'd expected. Yes, she'd been run through with a sword, the end of which still peeked through her abdomen, thick dark blood oozing from the wound. But the look of devastation on her face wasn't from the physical injury. It came from discovering who had delivered it.

"Massimo?" Luciana stumbled, reaching for the man who a few minutes ago, had been gazing at her like he had found a star fallen from the heavens. "Massimo, you… did *this* to me?"

Karahan pulled the shattered woman to his side. He looked at her, looked to Massimo, then back at her.

The Italian rolled to his feet. "You know this was justice, Karahan. You know what she did to my family!"

The Spatar's lips curled back. Without word, Karahan pulled the sword from the injured vampire's frame. He gave one disappointed look to Andreas, one gracious glance to Gerwalta, then swooped up the Doge in his arms and whipped through the courtyard.

Massimo turned his attention to Gerwalta. "You're bleeding."

"I'm…." She licked lips that had gone dry. "You saved me."

"And you saved us all."

"I…." She fell into Andreas's chest, wishing for warmth, for his arms wrapped protectively around her, and not the chill caused by so much blood loss.

"Gerwalta?" Andreas's hands threaded through her hair. "Someone help her!"

But what could be done? She was a dark one; her injury would heal, but that was only if she didn't bleed out first.

Her voice took on an ethereal quality, as though someone whispered in her own ears. "I love you, Andreas."

"I'll accept no farewells, love." His head lashed to the side. "Anyone, please!"

A flitter of black cloth fell in on her as one of the other wolfsretter appeared in her periphery. He muttered something, the words indistinct, as something cold stung her hemorrhaging wrist.

She closed her eyes and could not find the strength again to open them.

TWENTY-FOUR

Andreas was jealous of the fine silken linens tickling her form out of view. He wished it was his body wrapped around her, that he was claiming her as his heart and the animal within him ached to do. The patience he'd practiced during the year she kept from him strengthened his restraint.

But as her eyes fluttered open, love compelled him to her side. "Walta, how do you feel?"

"As though I've been preyed upon." Gerwalta's arm snaked out from under the blanket, examining her injured wrist. The silver Mehmet had affixed still held, the arm plate stemming the flow of blood and protecting the wound from corruption.

"Marvelous!" Gerwalta whispered, turning her arm to inspect all sides. "He actually managed to stitch together the damage… with silver. I have never seen our talents used this way."

"Yes, Mehmet was quite pleased with his work."

She wrapped her hand around the silver. "Sorry, who?"

"Mehmet. He's one of the hoods… the *wolfsretters* from the House of Night. Last night, after you passed out, he did that to stop the bleeding. He'd said you'd need to leave it on for a couple weeks."

Wolfsretter healed quickly, except from lupine bites. A consequence of opposing anatomy, he supposed. Where would the balance be if wolves suffered long from the burn of silver but their maw could do no more than render a temporary scratch? The burns Gerwalta had given him still ached, blistered bits of flesh across large parts of his body.

"Oh? I suppose there's no harm in that." Gerwalta shifted, her face screwing up. "Andreas?"

"Yes, my lamb?"

"Where are my clothes?" she asked. "Not that I am loathe, mind, to be without such ridiculous garb. Saints preserve me from the calamity of Venetian fashion."

Gerwalta put all her weight to her good side, pushing herself up in bed. "We are on a boat." Her eyes met his. "Whose?"

"It is an Ottoman trading ship."

Her eyes narrowed. "Are we here as guests or as prisoners?"

"Guests, though 'refugees' may be a more apt term. He let his mind wander for a moment before returning to the point. "Karahan has left the city, taking the deposed Doge with him, it seems. But this arrived just as we were pushing off port."

The wolf stood and drew a sheet of folded paper from his pocket. On its backside, a purple seal, one bearing a form of writing she did not recognize, but the image of a creature she did: an eight-legged dragon.

"Messer Mazzi received this," Andreas continued. "It was forwarded by one of his servants to us this morning, and in turn to them from Karahan.

Fraulein Faust,

Even as I recognize that you completed the task for which you were contracted, and at the result of injury, I know whatever payment or gratitude I have would not suffice. By ridding the world of the Ravens, you have done a service to vampires and wolves everywhere. As to the revelation of your ability to fly, however, there were simply too many witnesses for any amount of sway or collusion I could muster to contain such information. I am sorry, as I know this development will have a great number of consequences for you and Herr Baron. My offer stands: if ever you flee from the Schwarzwald and seek sanctuary, Inga (the deposed Doge and my blooded daughter) and I will welcome you in Navarre, where I am known as Ignacio Montana de Corazon. Sadly, it is time to let Spatar Goran Karahan fade into history. Such is the consequence of immortal existence; we must ever adapt to being someone new, and with each iteration, we become less ourselves. Who will *you become now? I hope I may meet her and have a chance to thank her in person.*

With deepest appreciations, Igor Khamarov, Paterfamilias of the Dracule Bloodline.

Andreas let the paper fall to the side, his eyes searching a nothingness between them.

Gerwalta's head worked through a slow bob. "Then I succeeded in capturing them all. What of the urns, then? What has become of them?"

"They came aboard with us." He licked his lips. "Walta, I wish to ask you something, and I trust you will give me nothing but the truth. Last night, many things occurred which may have led you to do and say things you might not otherwise—"

"You are wondering if I meant it when I called you my mate." She cut him off with a smile.

The konigswolf, however, thought the matter far too serious to be playful on the subject. "What Karahan said *is* true. Gossip runs before truth can put on its boots. Word will reach Triberg, and once they know what you can do, you will be the next Matron. It is a thing done; your fate is sealed."

Her head tilted to the side. "I thought you did not believe in fate."

"I do not believe that the divine sets before us a path we are obliged to walk, for what, then, would be the purpose of free will? But I *do* believe that debts may be drawn through tradition for which payments can only be paid or defaulted upon."

"I thought I had fallen in love with a wolf, and now I find a scholar beside my bed?" She shifted such that, if so inclined, he might see her bosom under her shift. Gerwalta's bosoms were works of art, though he admitted that might be the love talking.

"I am prepared, Andreas, to give my vow, my faith, and my body to you," she said. "I do not care what my mother or any of the wolfsretter *expect* of me. I let go such concerns when I embraced your love. Unless…." She pulled back, bringing the coverlet up under her chin. "Unless you no longer desire me? I did burn you with silver, but it was only to attempt to—"

He pressed his fingers against her mouth, stilling her words. Would that it was his lips instead, but he did not trust himself to stop when the only thing standing between them and consummation was consequence.

"Of course, I still desire you. I love you. You are the mate of my heart, and I will always love you. Only I have finally learned that you were right."

"What are you saying, Andreas?"

"I'm saying that our love does not render us immune to reality. You are amenable to me—"

"I am quite more than amenable. I would have you beneath me now if I could."

Lust ran through his veins, seized his nerves with a veracity no burn of silver could equal, and threatened to hijack his purpose. The konigswolf stood, putting distance between them. He *must* remain resolute. "Gerwalta, please, hear me out. Nothing would make me happier than to have you as my mate. But claiming you as my bride and denying all the wolves living under the dominion the benefit of your rule would be the epitome of selfishness on my part. As Matron, you would have the power not just to make *my* life better, but to set free from tyranny all the lupines in your region."

The red blaze of her cheeks deepened, but Gerwalta's passions were no longer set to intimacy. Rather, given the narrowing of her eyes, she might want to kill Andreas as much as kiss him.

Given the fire within him he struggled to douse, she could do the former by attempting the latter.

"You truly think that a Matron could so radically shift the flow of culture as to restructure our societies?" she demanded. "You would let our love die on the altar of something with no chance of coming true."

Shame weighted down his brow. "I would die for you, but I must live for my people. As must you."

She guffawed. "So, we're.... You're... I'm...."

"Lamb, please."

Suddenly, her words, her fretting, her tremoring hands… all ceased as her eyes fell upon him with steely determination. "My mother was right. Never trust a wolf."

Any silver she could wield his direction would never hurt as much as that statement.

"You know what is truly funny?" Gerwalta crossed her arms and lashed her gaze away. "After you were taken from Padua, I was going to rescue you. You and only you. But Karahan told me if I did as I'd been contracted to do, he would help us escape to somewhere where we could be together, man and wife. Everything I did last night was to win that for us. And I revealed my greatest secret, because I was fighting for *us.*"

What had he done? She loved him, openly proclaimed it, called him her mate. He'd campaigned for her heart, won it, then let it rot. He'd forgone his own happiness in anticipation of her benevolence for his pack, and in the process, turned her against them all.

Before he could utter a word in defense of his kind, the door behind them opened, filled by billowing, black robes. Mehmet took turns sizing both up. No doubt he could read the tension. If he knew of their argument, he said nothing on it. Instead, the wolfsretter waved a hand, saying "We need to speak. On deck, now," before abruptly turning to leave.

Gerwalta, shoulders squared, rose from the bed.

Andreas searched the space for something she might wear. "Walta, wait. You have barely a scrap of clothing on. Let me gather something for you to—"

She pushed by him, sparing him not a single glance. "A Matron-to-be needs no servant. And recall, Herr Baron, that as a wolfsretter, I am capable of seeing to my own."

With an exhale, her own cloak of heavy, crimson fabric fell over her shoulders and unto the ground, covering her form from the cold of night, and blocking him from the warmth of his affections.

TWENTY-FIVE

The midday sun shone overhead, offsetting the brisk seabreeze lacing fingers over the deck and through her hair. In the near-distance sat Venice, a black-and-gray pearl off the coast, its pink-hued tower, a pin placed by God to secure it in place.

Mehmet led them across the middeck to the rear of the ship, where the other wolfsretter and a woman of exquisite and exotic beauty stood. *The shewolf.* Her relaxed demeanor and unfamiliar attire made placing her familiarity somewhat difficult, but her gray eyes gave her away. But there was something else tugging at Gerwalta's instinct as well. The sense that there was another wolf—besides Andreas—in their proximity. Another below decks? Perhaps, only the sensation was more immediate, and somehow, unlike that any other wolf had ever given her.

It was the same sensation she'd had that night on the roof of Messer Mazzi's neighbor and again in the Doge's palace.

And then, as though she'd been struck by lightning, Gerwalta understood. She turned eyes on Ahmet. "He's an asenaic."

That had to be it. A wolf who was not a wolf, a wolfsretter who wasn't a wolfsretter. She'd never met one before, but what else would explain the inconsistent and abnormal sense she had around him. Ahmet was the child of a lupine and one of her own kind and that fact alone made his existence a crime.

Mehmet, at ease but a moment before, tensed. The long, twisted dagger he drew into existence gleamed in the light of day. The action, coupled with words in a foreign tongue, triggered the others to raise their guard as well. Suddenly, the asenaic bore two crescent blades which started as his wrist, arched outward, and curved back just below his elbow. His own arm served as handle. The shewolf, through some trickery or strategy, managed to pull herself within her robes in the manner of a turtle, before jutting out from the collapsing cloth in fully-fledged fur.

Even with the tension and urgency of the moment, Gerwalta

knew she needed to inquire on this design. It appeared these Turks had something to teach their German kin.

Mehmet held it to her chest. "How do you…?"

Gerwalta stole a quick look at Andreas, ready to urge restraint, only to find his eyes distant, his skin pale. She'd deal with the consequence of his broken heart later. For the moment, his shock numbed him at a convenient moment.

"Peace." She threw her hands into the air. "I do not wish to invite trouble. I have no cause to harm."

Andreas, though, had snapped from his trance. He pulled around her. "This is allowed in the dominion of the House of Night?"

Could this be the land Karahan had been speaking of? A place where a lupine and wolfsretter could be together and not fear persecution?

The tiny bubble of hope burst with Mehmet's averted gaze, the dagger gaining distance from her throat. "Encouraged? No. Tolerated with disdain? Yes. Hasan is a member of my House, but he has been disowned by our clan. As a wolf, however, he was accepted into Yasmin's pack. Until, that was, our Matron threatened to kill them all for harboring the dishonored."

Gerwalta's sympathies got the better of her. She tilted her head in the couple's direction, speaking although she knew the couple could not understand her words. "You were fleeing, looking for refuge." Then, turning back to Mehmet, she added, "but that doesn't explain your involvement."

Hasan spoke his foreign tongue behind them, the tone obvious despite the linguistic divide. After a few sentences, Mehmet hushed them.

"What?" Gerwalta asked. "What is he saying?"

"He is cursing Karahan," Mehmet said.

Andreas took a step back. "What of him?"

The wolfsretter hacked a laugh. "We are all here because of him. The vampire found us in Istanbul two months ago, said that if we helped him in the plot to overthrow the Doge and trap the Ravens, he would find us a place where we all could find sanctuary."

"And so you ended up in Venice?" Gerwalta asked. "True, there are no pack politics or wolfsretter Matrons to interrogate you, but such a city is no place for our kind. I felt tight in the chest the whole time I was there."

"No, it was not to Venice that he was to deliver us."

The mystery just grew deeper with every word the Turk said. "Then where were you going?"

"Isn't it obvious?" Andreas huffed. "They were on their way to Triberg."

Gerwalta whipped around. "Triberg? But why would they be heading…?"

But before the question was out of her mouth, her mind blended the loose clues into a whole.

Karahan's plan hinged on the inclusion of a wolfsretter, but he'd *already had* two involved from the House of Night. Yet, he'd come all the way from a distant empire to recruit *her*. He'd admitted during their sojourn that he'd learned of the relationship she had with Andreas from one of the wolves she'd rescued in Nuremberg. Was it so surprising if he'd known she could fly as well? She hadn't thought then that any of the wolves had witnessed it, but could she be certain?

"Karahan brought me here *because* he wanted me to be Matron." Had all the blood drained from her face? It must have. "He assumed I would have sympathy for an asenaic and a shewolf in love, because I was in love with a wolf myself. And if he gave me a task that could only be accomplished if a melee forced me to take flight…."

But that still left one thing unanswered.

Gerwalta shook her head. "That explains *them*," she pointed to Yasmin and Hasan, "but it doesn't explain *you*," she added, singling out Mehmet.

Andreas paced. "Let me fill that in then for you. Why else would a German-speaking Turk be heading for Triberg?"

If the konigswolf thought his rhetorical aside would bring clarity, he was sorely mistaken. But when Mehmet reached into his robe and pulled from it a bit of scroll bearing her mother's seal, it became clear.

"You were coming to compete for my hand."

"No, Fraulein, I was coming to *win* it," Mehmet said. "There hasn't been a hood born to the House of Night in five generations with the ability to fly. We fear that our bloodline has corrupted. But the House of Red…. For a century, each generation or two has been blessed. We seek to reseed our garden, in hopes some new trees may bear fruit. It was my intention to wed you and take you back to our home high in the Tarsus Mountains. Karahan never told me of the plot to make you Matron. He used me to his own ends, just as he used you."

Her pulse thundered in her ears. Gerwalta ran her good hand over her bad wrist, admiring the innovative silversmithing. Perhaps *her* bloodline had lost a few talents as well. "But it does not need be in vain."

For the first time, it was she who left Mehmet confused. "How so?"

If Andreas wanted her to be the Matron she didn't want to be for the good of his pack, then she'd assure the spouse she'd be forced to marry could be of like mind. "Yes, Karahan played us all, and we are all paying for that deceit. But how we got here doesn't matter. We must go forward with the consequences all the same. No, as a future Matron of the House of Red, I cannot return with you to your homeland, but our children could."

Mehmet's brow furrowed. "What of the ball and your mother's right to choose your husband for you?"

"In my opinion, she has sacrificed it by sending me off to become a vampire's puppet." She stepped forward before getting down on her knees. "Herr Mehmet, Righteous Wolfsretter of the House of Night, walk in night and hunt by moon with me. Offer me your fealty, and I will offer you my fidelity. Do you accept me as your bride, and will you consummate these, our vows, with your body in kind?"

He lifted an eyebrow. "What are you doing?"

"I am proposing marriage." Gerwalta went slack. "Was that not clear?"

Before Mehmet could answer, Andreas pulled her to her feet. "Walta, you cannot."

"Why not?" she snapped. "You said you will not have me, that I am of more use to you as a Matron than a mate. So be it. I will wed Mehmet and become Matron, just as you wished. Can you doubt that your pack will be treated better under our combined rule than someone my mother would pick? Look how he fought to protect a shewolf and asenaic!"

"But when I said I would not marry you I did not mean that you should marry…."

His arguments snuffed under the collapse of his own logic. Gerwalta pushed the stunned konigswolf aside, making her way toward her suddenly betrothed.

"I have one request, though, Herr Mehmet." She took to her feet. "We must wed immediately."

Even the Ottoman wolfsretter seemed dumbfounded at the success of his own campaign. "You do not need more time than that to prepare?"

"Would time bring us another choice? If anything, it dissolves this one we are to make. Word of my ability to fly will reach Triberg well before I do. My mother will quickly align a new path for me, and considerations of what I desire will find no welcome in her hands. But you must swear to me that you will never speak a word to anyone what I said to Herr Baron last evening. I will have your oath that you will do everything within your power, if rumors fester, to deny, and to uphold his good standing and keep him from harm."

"It is to my advantage to do so. I would not live in a foreign land *and* be branded a cuckhold." Mehmet's eyes focused on the wolf beside her as he withdrew his silver at last. "But you must also agree that this romance of yours ends today. My compassion for the wolves does not extend to one sharing my wedding bed."

The black-cloaked man looked at her, then at Andreas, and back at her. He held out his weapon hand.

Gerwalta took a deep breath, swallowed her heart, and reached out in kind.

And that was when they heard the splash.

Four bodies rammed into the railing of the ship in unison, taking in the sight. Andreas did not look back as he paddled——had he taken his wolf because it made the swim easier?—back toward the mainland.

"Andreas, you fool!" Gerwalta cried. "The tides will sweep you out to sea. Come back! Come back this very minute."

The konigswolf stayed true to his path.

Which, it seemed, was far away from her.

TWENTY-SIX

Gerwalta stood dumbfounded in the slayer's foyer, holding out the pouch of refused silver.

"What do you mean you have no use for it?" she asked. "At the very least, take it on behalf of your neighbor whose roof Andreas crashed through. We owe them repairs."

"Massimo has already made arrangements to have the damage repaired." Mazzi waved off her concern. "I am sorry that Karahan left without upholding his end of your agreement; it feels inappropriate asking you for anything in return. Tell me, will it be difficult for you to return to the Schwarzwald?"

She looked away. "It was foolish of me to suppose I could hide something so immense forever. Now that my ability to fly is known, there is nothing for me to do. At least my increased influence will be a boon for the lupines."

Mazzi chuckled. "I'm not talking about your flight. I mean your love for Herr Baron. Not many may have been able to understand the German you spoke to each other, but your eyes spoke more loudly than your words. Everyone in that room could see the heat between you as you fought for each other."

Terror pulled at the tendrils of her heart. "It does not matter. I have offered my hand to one of the wolfsretters from the House of Night, and he has accepted."

"One of the…. Your hand…." Mazzi struggled to find meaning in her words. "Surely you jest."

"I do not. We will exchange vows tonight before departing for Triberg."

Though thank grace they had agreed to delay the consummation until they reached Schloss Wolfsretter. Gerwalta may be bold enough to make her own match, but even she wouldn't dare to close out the finalities without her mother's approval. Not if she wanted to become Matron and not be banished on the spot. To that end, she had agreed that she would arrive to Triberg first and alone to deliver the news of her betrothal. She did not know Mehmet well, but she did not wish him harm. If Gunda Faust wished to fume over her fourth daughter's bold acts, she'd take the brunt of the flames alone.

The Ottoman contingent would arrive the next day. Gerwalta could only hope that Andreas would have returned by then, and that he'd be willing to accept Hasan and Jasmine to his pack. She'd like to have said she had no doubt of it; his compassion, like that he'd shown to the wolf sent on his king orders to slay her, was one of the things she loved about him.

Mazzi, however, was Italian. "But you love Andreas," he persisted.

"It matters not," she said. "Please, Messer Mazzi, believe me. I am heartsick over the whole affair, but I am doing what I must to protect us all. Do not salt my wounds."

The old man relented. "Then I wish you happiness, Fraulein Faust. As much of it as you're able to grasp."

The Matron's scowl came as no surprise. "How could you not tell me?"

There was no need to ask what. "I am a fourth daughter, a fifth child. I did not reveal that I could fly because I did not think myself worthy of being Matron. It is rightfully Helga's—"

Her mother bore down on her, a hand encircling Gerwalta's throat. "Who succeeds me is my decision. Both you and Helga need to remember that."

Her voice cracked from the pressure on her larynx. "Yes, Matron."

"And withholding this knowledge was an attempt by you to usurp that right."

"Yes, Matron. I can only beg your forgiveness."

Her mother released her hold, sending Gerwalta to the floor. "No, you do not. A Matron never begs. Learn this and learn it now,

Gerwalta. It is only the first lesson I must teach you. That I should have spent *years* teaching you. We have so much now to cover." She shook her head. "So many years wasted on Helga."

Gerwalta lifted her head, looking across the faces of her family, gathered to learn the news of her return. Helga's eyes blazed. It lasted only a moment, etching away by bitterness directed squarely at her little sister.

Any fear she'd felt before? It reverberated in that icy stare.

But the Matron wasn't done. "Not only have you spent years keeping secrets, but now you have gone and arranged your own marriage? Tell me truly, daughter, are there any more secrets waiting for my discovery?"

She bit her tongue. The only one remaining would go with her to the grave.

Gerwalta searched the dust on the floor for her next words, wondering what she should do to quell her mother's anger. "No, mother."

Gunda crossed her arms and pursed her lips. "Good. Then let us proceed. Helga!"

Stunned that her presence was even recalled, the Matron's first daughter snapped to attention. "Yes, Mother?"

Gunda's arm lashed to the side, her finger extending to the outer walls of the castle. "Order the fires built for tomorrow night and send word to those who've already arrived for the ball that it has instead become a wedding feast."

"The… fires, Matron?" Helga, perplexed, looked to Gerwalta for guidance. "But *fauernacht* is not for another two nights."

"Did I stumble in my speech? Or do you think I am unaware of when comes the full moon?" The Matron did not wait for her first born to answer. "Your sister has made a mockery of this family, and we need amend it immediately. Tonight, she and her wedded will make good on their oaths. Do you hear me, Gerwalta? You will consummate your union and go about making yourself into a worthy heir."

She swallowed her fear. "Yes, Matron."

TWENTY-SEVEN

Gerwalta stared at herself in the looking glass, wondering who stared back. Surely this woman who she saw could not become a matron? But then again, was this not the woman who'd broken the heart of the man she loved, not once, but twice? Wasn't it she who usurped her mother's place in selecting a husband? Was it not she who had trapped the seven deadly vampires whose silver urns now were shelved in the wine cellar below?

Was she not the woman who was about to make love to a man she barely even knew to solidify her ability to carry out her own agenda? Perhaps Mehmet also looked with dread upon the act they were about to undertake. After all, he'd readily agreed to delaying consummation instead of demanding it as his right. Maybe he found her disgusting, and they'd never have one mote of the passion she and Andreas had, that the act of creating children would be a necessary chore they'd both slog through out of duty, and that his company and consort would cease when she'd born enough children.

It was happening; she was becoming her mother.

In the bailey below, the wedding guests reveled. A few, perhaps, with somewhat less exuberance. After all, they'd come to the Schwarzwald believing they'd be competing for her hand, only to be informed it had already been awarded. Gerwalta was no expect in marital matters, but she did not believe starting out with so many slighted would-be suitors boded well for Mehmet and herself. Whatever, such cares would have to wait for later. For the moment, her only concern was that she needed to descend and claim her husband.

She let slip her shift and summoned her red cloak, making it somewhat longer than usual so it draped about her feet and touched the ground. This was tradition: the bride wore only her colors into the tent. Her husband would remove it and place it on his own shoulders, signifying his acceptance into her clan. Then he would summon *his* cloak to wrap around her before they both removed them and… well, the rest was simply fornication, wasn't it?

Gerwalta took each step down from her room with deliberation, focusing on what need be done. A shift in her periphery stopped her, and she turned just in time to duck, sending Helga flying over her and landing at the bottom of the stairs.

Her sister was a gifted warrior; only a fool would deny that. She landed rough but in a skilled manner, quickly recovering, summoning a blade and awaiting.

"Helga, do not blame me for this," her sister begged. "I hid it as long as I could. I never wanted to usurp your claim to the throne."

"Oh, do not worry little sister, you haven't," Helga spat back, her blond tresses shaking with each word spit out. "Our sainted mother is in good health, with many years left in her body. That gives me plenty of time."

Gerwalta held her arms out, brandishing her chest. "Run me through now, then. I have no silver. Even my medallion has been left upstairs. I am defenseless."

"Do you think me a fool?" Helga spit back. "Everyone would know it was me. I would never be so stupid as to kill you myself."

"What will you do then? Conscript another konigswolf within our region to send one of his wolves to kill me? It must have so upset you when you learned your hopeful assassin failed to carry out his orders."

A half-cocked grin pulled up Helga's sinister lips. "As much as it would upset you, I'd wager, to learn that that wolf never made it back to the Schwarzwald."

Gerwalta blanched. "How…?"

"Do you really think I put all my eggs in one basket, little one? Remember that mother has spent years training me for the position I am due: I have networks of spies all over our region, and even far beyond it. In fact…" Helga drew her sword to her open palm, examining its edge. "You may be surprised what I know. Great Aunt Maria was."

So Gerwalta's suspicions had been well founded. Helga *had* killed Maria Dreger. But that wasn't what struck fear into the heart of the young wolfsretter as much as the greater implication of what her sister had just professed.

"What do you know?"

Helga lowered her sword. "You should run along now, Gerwalta. Your betrothed will be pulsing with anticipation. I don't know if anyone's ever told you. Although we women are the superior sex, our men are so much more... *licentious* than we are. They love coupling, need it even. You'll learn, when you go now and let your bridegroom partake of you, how the act of making love means so much to them." She balanced her chin on an index finger. "Oh, dear, I bet Herr Baron is in shambles tonight, knowing the wolfsretter he loves is in the arms of another. Of course, I know you never *consummated* your relationship with him. If you had, he'd be here tonight, trying to kill Mehmet. I wonder, if I were to wander down to the packlands while your performing your wifely duties, and bound the konigswolf, if I might bring him some *comfort*. Like I said, males love coupling. Their bodies sometimes *rise* to the call, even when their heart is distant."

Gerwalta's hands curled so tightly into fists beneath her cloaks, pearls of hot blood pooled under her fingernails. "You wouldn't."

"Would it grieve you if I claimed your beloved's virginity, leaving him bonded to me?" Helga mocked. "Leaving him *in love* with me?"

"You hate me, sister, but you hate werewolves more. Enough with your empty threats. You would never *touch* a lupine with anything but derision."

Helga claimed the space remaining between them. "You're right, I wouldn't. But now that you've confirmed with your anger what my spies reported to me, I have all the evidence I need to kill Andreas Baron." She leaned in, whispering, "with complete legitimacy."

Gerwalta wanted silver. She wanted to kill Helga where she stood, but the consequences facing Helga were the same ones forestalling Gerwalta.

Helga backstepped her way down the stairs. "But don't worry, little sister. I'll make it look like an accident. After all, I can't have the satisfaction of killing you later if I expose your sins and get you banished now, can I? In fact, you should thank me for disposing of the powder keg that the konigswolf represents. Go to your *rightful* husband. I have things to do, and I cannot depart until you are riding your husband inside that tent out there. I should return to the castle by morning with a glorious wedding present."

With that, Helga left.

Gerwalta didn't move. Couldn't move. Couldn't force her feet to obey. What to do? *What to do?* Did Helga mean it? Even she would know the dangers of killing the pack's king unprovoked. Even if it was made to look like an accident, rumors and unrest would plague the lot. Was Helga the kind who wouldn't care, as long as any arising crisis gave her opportunity to hurt her own little sister.

Of course, she was.

Stepping forward would be the same as walking Andreas to the gallows. Retreating upstairs, the same as if she slew him herself.

She lifted a foot…

…and pivoted.

Gerwalta dashed up the stairs, across the throne room, to the base of the tower. She had no silver to mold stairs, but she didn't need. With a flex of her legs, she rose into the air, ascending. She couldn't flee through the bailey, of course. The wedding guests would have their eyes fixed on the door leading from the castle, ready to cheer her emergence and escort her to the tent where Mehmet waited. The only way she could get to Andreas in time was if she flew, and the only way to get out of the castle unseen was through the tower.

She only hoped that Helga did not realize what she'd done until it was too late, and that when she got to the packlands in the valley below, she could convince Andreas to run for his life.

TWENTY-EIGHT

She found him in the field, alone, chopping wood by the dim light of a small blaze he'd built for utlity.

He would know she was there; such was the nature between wolfsretters and lupines. The konigswolf, however, gave her arrival no pause except to still a single moment, before reaching to the pile of lumber beside him and picking up another log.

"Go away."

"Herr Konigswolf, you must to listen to me."

Swing. *Thwack!*

"Helga is coming. She means to kill you."

Thwack!

"You must flee now. Make for Navarre. Seek sanctuary with Karahan."

Thwack!

"Why aren't you moving already? Andreas!"

He raised the axe overhead, but this time, before he could bring its weight down upon the log he'd positioned, she rounded on him. Gerwalta pushed her arms to his biceps and her stare to the depths of his soul.

"Did you not hear what I said? Run, Andreas. Save yourself."

The tremor in his arms could have been because of any number of things: the weight of the blade frozen in an odd position, the lure of swinging forward and pushing her away in the process, the temptation to drop all and claim her lips. . . .

His words were hoarse. "Save myself for what? I have lost you. What have I to live for?"

"What have you to live for?" She motioned vaguely to the trail that led back to his homestead. "Every wolf who calls this valley home, that's what. The land that you and your pack have tended for generations. The hopes of a mate who will give you strong daughters and handsome sons. You have everything to live for."

The wolf threw the axe to the ground as he turned away. "I thought so too when I jumped off that boat. I told myself I would live for only them, for my pack. But what am I now? I am no king who can lead. I am pup who followed a moth to the flame and was burned in the fire."

He turned over his shoulder, looking toward her, but not at her. "You should leave, Frau Faust. If your sister is truly coming to kill me, perhaps it is a mercy to us both. You can move on with your life, and I can stop treading endless still waters in mine. Go, Gerwalta. Go home to your mate."

She stepped up behind him, putting her hand on his shoulder and leaning her chin against his back. "I need not go anywhere to see my mate. He's right here."

Andreas turned, grinning. "Pretty words, but you already have a husband, do you not?"

Another three steps to circle him. Gerwalta laid one hand on his chest, and the other behind his neck, pulling herself up to him. "I only proposed to him because I was angry at you for pushing me to be Matron. A foolish act of momentary insult. The moment Helga said she was coming to kill you, I knew I'd rather be the cause of your death than the one who costs you your life. If you're prepared to die either way, at least die in my arms, Andreas. I pledge myself to you and only you. I am *your* mate, forever."

Her eyes closed as she drew herself to him, but moments from his lips, his words stilled her.

"I will ask one last time, and you must be certain: am I who and what you want forever, knowing what it means for us both? If we do this, I will be *bound* to you."

The wolfsretter paused, pulling back just enough to frame him in her vision. "I know what I want."

He grinned. "Do you?" Andreas's left hand circled around, finding the curve of her backside and filling his palm with it. Meanwhile, his right hand crept up her ribs, drifting lithely, until it found the swell of her unbound breast beneath the cloak, closing over it, squeezing it in the most delightful way.

Oh, sweet agony.

Gerwalta's hands clutched at the collar of his jacket, holding herself as even the teasing of her breast weakened her knees. His head tilted like that of a puppy when she unwound herself from him, and she saw the concern weigh in his eyes. Was she again changing her mind? Would she deny him? But apprehension turned to appetite when she drew in a deep breath before letting it out in a gentle push. The magic that summoned her cloak ebbed, dissolving the garment into nothingness.

His eyes clung to her naked form, even as the dew of night began to fall upon her. She veritably stalked him, each step languid, her hips swinging as she navigated the uneven forest floor.

"It's you, Andreas." Gerwalta's hand cupped his cheek. "I only want you."

It was such an odd reversal: she, the one raised to contain and hide, presenting herself to the world red cloak-first, to be without it in his sight. He, from a people who treated nudity as common fashion, obfuscated from sight, suddenly struck dumb by her exposure.

Andreas leaned in, treating her to a taste, a mere brush of lip on lip, a tentative first step in the dance that lay before them. Gerwalta raised her other hand, holding his face in her grasp.

"Andreas Baron, Konigswolf of the Schwarzwald Pack, walk in night and hunt by moon with me. Offer me your fealty, and I will offer you my fidelity. Do you accept me as your bride, and will you consummate these, our vows, with your body in kind?"

He blinked. "These are the same words you said to Mehmet."

"The vow is not binding until the union is consummated."

"You mean you have not…." His words died away. Andreas took her face in his hands, drawing her lips to his. "I accept. Even if you *had* been with him, I'd accept. My love has no qualifications."

Gerwalta gasped as the konigswolf swept her from her feet, carrying her with all the ease of a bear lifting a twig. "Is there not some lupine custom you wish me to uphold?"

"We don't use words." He walked her away from the shattered, split pile of logs and toward a patch of untouched snow. "We take action."

Frost bit her skin as he laid her upon the ground, a contrast to the heat building within her. Andreas's eyes stayed locked in hers as he pulled off his coat and let it fall away, soon joined therein by his shirt, his breeches, his boots. Her eyes had feasted on his form before, but never with so much anticipation. He paused over her, taking a moment to breathe before falling to his knees.

"The snow?" He said, curling one hand behind her neck and pulling her lips to his. "Does it bother you?"

She let the act play out languidly, slowly using their connection to draw him back. "I am a dark one; it causes no offense." Her head flattened, her long auburn hair pooling underneath and providing something in the way of a pillow. "Besides, I find myself quite warm."

Andreas's weight settled over her, molding the winter landscape beneath to her form. He laughed into her neck as he nuzzled. "We may melt the whole forest before we're through."

His mouth explored her, moving with aching clarity down her neck, dotting kisses across her chest, until he wrapped his lips around the rise of her breast. Gerwalta threw her head back, sucking in breath, even as he moved his attentions from left to right.

"I will make you happy, Walta," he mumbled as he found his way back to her mouth, demanding her kiss. His body shifted, leaving his manhood crested upon the pulsation of her desire, teasing her with promise. "I swear it."

With one last look, he sought permission. Gerwalta suppressed her frustration, wanting him to take what was so clearly his, but understood that the next moment would seal his heart to hers. He could never walk away.

She nodded, preparing herself for the initial discomfort her sisters had harked on about behind folded hands. Andreas's hips rolled with aching slowness, as the pressure of his entrance pressed in on her. Gerwalta bit her lip; the stories had not been wholly false, and she suddenly wondered if the enjoyable part of this practice had all been a lie. The konigswolf let out a slow moan, pausing when he was fully sheathed within her. With a deep breath, the tightness of her frame eased, and yet, he did not move. His head stay buried in the crux of her neck and shoulder.

"Andreas?"

No answer, no movement save for his breathing.

"Andreas, are you all right?"

His head jerked up, revealing feral eyes. *Lupine* eyes. Eyes that had found prey and sized it up for eating.

"I… I love you." He'd said it before, but never like this. Never with such… awe. His hand rose to stroke back her hair. "Walta, I love you."

"And I love y—Oh. *Ohh…*"

Her words stilled as his passion unleashed. Suddenly, their exchange transformed from serene and sacred to ferocious and animalistic.

And she found she quite liked it.

Andreas's hands curled under her, clutching her shoulders from behind. He used her as an anchor, pulling himself deeper with each thrust. And with each thrust, a grunt, a growl, a heated pulse of his lupine nature. Gone was the anxiety and the discomfort. Gerwalta fought her own nature that screamed at her to dominate this man, this creature. The woman within her knew there was so much more promise in ceding control.

He waxed and waned, the cycles of the moon playing out between her thighs. They ceased being separate creatures as she felt the shift. It seemed impossible; a wolfsretter didn't *bond*, but the emotions that invaded her as he worked into her… What else *could* it be called but bonding?

And suddenly, she realized: love. It was love that was swelling up within her.

In a blink, the physical grabbed attention away from her emotions. Her insides coiled, even as Andreas pushed into her so hard, he moved her across the ground in the process of claiming her.

"Walta, I'm…."

But his words cut off as she called out, her body reverberating with feeling. One moment, every muscle within her clenched as though struck by lightning, every nerve electrocuted. The next, her body went limp, a sense of euphoria flooding her from head to foot. It was everything she had felt the first time, but more so and deeper. Within a few more strokes built to a crescendo, Andreas growled, almost howled, before falling atop of her, destroyed by his own efforts.

They rested there, in the snow under the trees, as though eminent danger did not grow closer by the moment. Andreas's arm hooked out to gather her close as he rolled onto his side. He turned to kiss her forehead, folding her arms in between them. His hands worked the tangles of her hair as Gerwalta recalled her cloak into being, untying it at the neck and using it as a blanket to cover them both.

"It is done, then," Andreas huffed, struggling to catch his breath. "Now what?"

Gerwalta pushed herself up on the palm of her hand and reached for him with another. She leaned in, brushing a kiss to his lips. "Now, we run."

TWENTY-NINE

Triberg had not impressed Mehmet, that was for certain.

As he awaited his bride, he recalled his initial impression upon arrival. Was this what passed for a fortress in these parts? One measly tower that didn't rise but five floors? A scattering of odd, mismatched buildings trapped into a compound by the presence of irregular stone walls hardly tall enough to keep out a squirrel, let alone a vampire? A throne room that would be lucky to hold fifty people, and a courtyard that struggled to hold two hundred?

Venice hadn't suited him either, frankly. At least the Doge's Palace was large enough to host a proper party, though. If there was one thing Mehmet had learned from the laity of Istanbul, it was that: largess demands authority. Authority demands power. Power demands whatever it wants.

If Schloss Wolfsretter did not demand authority, then he would have to seize it through ruthlessness, cunning, and guile.

All of which would be aided by wedding Gerwalta Faust. As a *kushan,* a hood who could fly, she would become her bloodline's next Matron. As a fourth daughter and barely into her birthright, she was young enough to be brought to heel. He'd oversee her furthering education and have her eating from his hand. It did not hurt that she was an attractive little thing. He was so going to enjoy stripping her of her innocence.

If only she would come down from her quarters in this poor excuse of a castle to let him do as much! He'd put off on the trip to Triberg, using concern for her mother's approval, until he was certain her family and her lands had enough potential to exploit. He did not favor his bride's schloss, but those silver mines which ran through the dominion of the House of Red? They were worth the arrangement.

And it hadn't been a lie, what he told her; there hadn't been a *kushan* born in the House of Night for decades. If he could return to barter children with the potential: he'd rule both east and west, even if by proxy, achieving the goal that fool Bernhard Dreger had planned and failed at.

The air inside the tent shifted, a slash of winter darting through the space heated by the brazier burning within. *Time to pull back on the masque of innocence*, he thought.

"You made me nervous, Gerwalta. I was beginning to fear that you'd changed your mind."

When he turned, however, he found not his betrothed, her red hair falling languidly over her milky white shoulders, but her eldest sister, the reincarnation of a northern goddess.

Helga held a silver staff poised to strike, but he stayed his reaction. She might have causes that had nothing to do with him. No such luck. Within moments, she had the weapon kissing his throat.

"Are you party to her betrayal?"

Mehmet blinked his confusion. "Whose? What?"

"Gerwalta, you fool! I have just heard back from my spies in Venice. They say that not only did she openly declare Andreas Baron her mate, but that *you* assisted her in escaping the city in the aftermath of the coup."

Was that the way of it? Sister spying on sister? Helga must have known the Matron's fourth-born posed a threat to her claim on the throne, then. She'd want to take her down, and if that happened *before* he'd consecrated their union, all the work and sacrifice of these last months would be for naught.

Mehmet lowered his masque, pushing Helga's sword away with a delicately placed finger tip. "Escape is a bit of an overstatement, Frau Faust. I *isolated* her."

Helga posture softened. "Isolated her? To what end?"

"To exploit her, of course." He held his hands aloft, indicting their surroundings. "You do not seriously believe I would compete to win this, do you? To be son to the House of Red and have a fourth-born daughter as my bride? No, my ambitions are a bit *bigger*." He dared a step forward. "As I believe yours are, too."

"I wish to be Matron of the House of Red," she snapped,

dropping the staff in a huff of frustration. "That is no secret."

When she backed into the central post holding the tent up, Helga dropped the sword.

Mehmet stepped into her, drifting a finger over her chin. "No, *bigger.*" He focused on her lips.

The muscles of her face tightened, but she did not back away. "What are you doing, Herr Mehmet? I am the sister of your betrothed."

"And where *is* my betrothed?" he asked, already knowing the answer.

Helga's throat twitched as she swallowed. "I know not."

"Of course, you do. *I* do. She's gone to Baron. As disgusted as I was by their romance, I do not think it false. Their attraction was evident to all who saw them. I wouldn't be surprised to learn that he's defiling her even now."

A smile ticked up on Helga's face. "You would have cause for retaliation if so."

"Yes, I would." Finally, some progress. "But surely I'd want more for enduring such an insult than the head of the konigswolf." He drew a line down her chin, her neck, tapering off right above her breast. "I have big plans, Helga. Far bigger than the Schwarzwald, though it's a start. What about you? How big can you dream?"

"I already have a husband."

An obstacle, but not one that couldn't be overtaken. "He should accompany me to the packlands tonight, but he should know the mission will be dangerous. Killing a whole pack is not for the faint of heart."

Helga's chest rose and fell with increased effort. "I will send for him directly."

"Good. Then I will gather my silver and make my way immediately. Tell me, Frau Faust, where will I find their encampment?"

"The pack shares a farmstead in the valley. It is over the river and through the woods."

He kept their eyes locked as he kneeled, picking up the weapon she'd abandoned. In his hands, the metal transformed, closing in on itself, thickening, condensing, until where a staff had been, only an axe remained.

"Tell your mother I will return with Baron's head and her daughter in chains."

Helga cocked her head to the side. "You will let Gerwalta live?"

"Of course. Killing the pack will make every lupine fear me. You and I killing your sister together, however? That will make *every dark one* fear *us*."

Coming Late Fall 2019:
Red & the Restorer – Red Hood Origins #3

The Red Hood Origins is a prequel to the contemporary fairy-tale-inspired urban fantasy series, The Red Hood Chronicles.

www.ingramcontent.com/pod-product-compliance
Lightning Source LLC
Chambersburg PA
CBHW050145110726
47898CB00008B/2681